Locking Horns . . .

Sean made a disgusted sound. "You think it's that easy? Sean Alexander failed in front of a nation and his ego couldn't handle it?"

"You had to be dragged onto this case, didn't you?" And Jennifer knew she'd revealed too much by the quick way he looked at her, by the absolute cynicism in his smile.

"So, it's true what they say about you. Tell me, Special Agent Bennett, were you hand-picked? Did you agree to come on board, not because the life of an innocent ten-year-old is at stake, but rather because maybe this is your big chance?"

Stung because she couldn't fully deny it, Jennifer said, "Go to hell."

"Lady, I've already been there. And if your wide eyes can't let you imagine what I'm really talking about, we *will* have a problem."

FINAL HOUR

Tracey Tillis

AN ONYX BOOK

ONYX
Published by the Penguin Group
Penguin Putnam Inc., 375 Hudson Street,
New York, New York 10014, U.S.A.
Penguin Books Ltd, 27 Wrights Lane,
London W8 5TZ, England
Penguin Books Australia Ltd, Ringwood,
Victoria, Australia
Penguin Books Canada Ltd, 10 Alcorn Avenue,
Toronto, Ontario, Canada M4V 3B2
Penguin Books (N.Z.) Ltd, 182–190 Wairau Road,
Auckland 10, New Zealand

Penguin Books Ltd, Registered Offices:
Harmondsworth, Middlesex, England

First published by Onyx, an imprint of Dutton NAL,
a member of Penguin Putnam Inc.

First Printing, April, 1999
10 9 8 7 6 5 4 3 2 1

 REGISTERED TRADEMARK—MARCA REGISTRADA

Printed in the United States of America

Chapter One

Day One
Central Indiana

The two in the special delivery truck had no idea they were being followed.

The occupants of the blue Buick four door were relatively sure of this because in the half hour they'd been tracking the truck, the vehicle hadn't deviated from its scheduled routine.

The Freightliner truck that had pulled out of Milo's Furniture and Collectibles at seven forty-five a.m. hadn't dropped below or exceeded the speed limit at any time before or during its twenty-minute stretch along the city beltway.

No moving aside to let the Buick pass, no slowing down or pulling back to check out the Buick's drivers. It sailed obliviously on at a steady rate of sixty, more or less. Only the occasional flash of a red cap, pale face, and blond hair from the driver's side-view mirror and a corresponding flash of dark hair and pale features from the passenger's mirror teased the two men in the Buick.

According to the dispatch schedule, the van was making good time to delivery number two.

The Buick followed two cars behind to an exit ramp that spilled them onto a state road on the west side of Indianapolis.

Because they were in the heart of an industrial district, the small stream of early-morning traffic surrounding them took on an addition of slow-moving big rig convoys and tankers. The trucks slowed everyone down while they made a crisscrossing series of entrances and exits along interstates entering and leaving the city.

At a red light at the bottom of the ramp, still two cars behind the delivery truck, the Buick waited patiently.

When traffic moved forward again, the Buick's driver glanced in the rearview mirror. Family luxury vans and small sport utility trucks, filled with chattering couples and bouncing kids, snaked all the way back to the interstate. He knew that as the morning grew long, the number of recreational travelers would increase.

Fall in Indiana drew heavy tourist crowds, especially to its rural southern towns. The blazing patchwork of turning trees melded with Indian summer temperateness to provide a cozy seduction for visitors.

The two in the Buick didn't need it, didn't need the numbers today, given the sensitive job they were en route to carry out.

The light turned green. The truck, leading the line of traffic now, lumbered through the intersection. It turned left onto a southbound state road. The Buick followed in silence for another twenty minutes.

"Eight-fifteen," Roy commented, adjusting the car's rearview mirror.

"Yeah?" his partner Hal answered.

"Little early."

"We're okay." A few seconds passed. "What if something goes wrong?"

"It won't."

"How come you're so sure. Something can *always* go wrong."

"Have we had problems yet?"

"That's not—"

"Why should we now?"

Hal sighed.

"It's moving like clockwork." Roy touched the pistol tucked inside the hip pocket of his nylon vest.

Hal caught the movement. He felt reassured by his own weapon.

A green county line marker came up on their right,

signaling their exit from Johnson County and entrance into Morgan County. Twelve minutes after that, the delivery truck pulled off onto an older rutted, two-lane road.

They would kill the boy if they had too. She didn't get any kicks out of that possibility. But they'd all discussed it last night when they'd left her house, less than a mile's walk from here. She accepted it. She was a practical woman.

The road was still empty all the way down to where it T'd into the old state road that bisected it. She glanced at her watch. Less than ten minutes to go. She walked over to the bundle she'd placed at the foot of the tree deep inside the woods. She knelt down to the heap of cloth, spread it all out, then started unbuttoning her blouse.

"Charles Lattimore, I said no." Paul Lattimore crossed his arms over his broad chest and stood tall. The ex-senator hoped his imposing six-foot-two height, which occasionally had stood him in advantageous stead on Capitol Hill, looked suitably imposing to his young son. He doubted it, catching the light in the boy's eye.

In fact, Charlie Lattimore recognized his father's stern-faced tactic and eyed the screen door behind his back. He weighed his options. He loved his father, respected him enough to want to obey him. But a peek at his watch showed him he didn't have time, or a choice.

"Dad, where would I go? There's a big fence with a guard behind it. I just want to get out for a little while," he hesitated, "to, you know."

Paul Lattimore deflated.

Charlie stood mentally tough against his father's dejection. The gazebo was *his* place, behind the house, near the woods. It had been *their* special place—his and his mother's—before she had died. His father had never intruded while she was living. Charlie appreciated the way his father still didn't when he wished to be alone there with her memory.

He wished he could explain to his father why something more than memory called him there now. But *she'd* told him not to, told him no one would believe him if he revealed the truth.

She called herself his mother. She said she would be at the gazebo waiting for him.

Of course, it was stupid to believe she really was his mother. His father and the therapist who was treating him had convinced him she really was gone. Even though she sometimes appeared to him in his dreams.

So why these phone calls now from the woman whose voice was his mother's yet *not* his mother's? The things she told him, only they alone had shared.

She said she needed to do more than talk to him, she needed to prove to him that she had come back . . .

"Get your coat, son. It only looks like summer out there."

Charlie lifted a hand as he detoured to the hall closet. His mind was already on the gazebo, the woman, the woods.

"What's that?" John Paine geared the delivery truck into neutral. A woman stood in the middle of the road, waving her arms. There was no car in sight, though she was clearly in some sort of distress.

Sympathizing with whatever was the problem—no doubt some lone-woman motorist's worst nightmare—John stopped the truck. He thought, what if his own wife, pregnant no less, fell into the same predicament and needed some stranger's help? His partner, Jimmy Martins, already had his hand on the door handle, ready to get out.

Neither of them even saw the two men coming. One minute they were preparing to help the woman, the next, they were looking at guns pressed to their windows, pointed at their heads.

"What the hell—!" Jimmy's hand slipped off the handle to his thigh.

John barely heard him. He was looking back at the woman, who now appeared to be miraculously self-possessed. Robbery? No one traveled this road. At least, no more often than maybe once every few hours. There were no houses along this stretch. There were no houses even close. It was just a tree-lined shortcut that joined the interstate to the semiprivate road they'd often traveled on delivery runs before.

They'd actually looked forward to the detour this morning, with the leaves turning so pretty. Dammit, *dammit*!

The two men tapped the windows with their guns, motioning for John and Jimmy to get out.

John saw his wife's face in his mind's eye, smiling at him across their breakfast table.

"John, what—?"

John couldn't think what Jimmy expected him to do. Slowly, he opened his door and stepped down onto the pavement. It occurred to him Jimmy was only twenty, half his age. Jimmy was only a kid.

Roy caught Hal's eye through the passenger's window. "Get him over here."

Hal motioned with the gun and Jimmy preceded him around the front of the truck to where Roy and John stood. John and Jimmy exchanged uneasy looks. Hal saw Jimmy swallow.

Roy prodded John in the back with his gun and they all started walking toward the woman.

"Do we take the car?" she asked Roy when they reached her.

7

"Isn't far enough."

"And the stuff's in the back?"

"Where I put it last night. Hal?" Roy shifted his gun from John to Jimmy, then back to John again, to remind them he still had them covered.

Hal walked to the back of the Buick and opened the trunk. He took out an oilcloth satchel about as long as a golf bag. It was zipped shut. He hoisted the bag over his shoulder and rejoined Roy. When his gun was on Jimmy again, Roy ordered, "Judy, get it off the road."

Judy eyed the shallow embankment, calculating the difficulty of navigating the car down the decline and into the tangle of bushes beyond. After a moment, she nodded back at Roy, seemingly unperturbed.

Roy waved his gun. "Hal, gentlemen. Judy'll catch up."

The men walked for about twenty yards down the road. No cars came into sight. The distant traffic on the road running parallel to this one was only an occasional rising and fading swish.

Roy knew if somebody happened along chances were better than good they'd just assume the truckers had pulled off to the side for a nap. Nothing uncommon about that along highways and connecting side roads. And there was nothing suspicious about the delivery truck as long as it didn't sit here forever.

At a sprawling birch tree, whose leaf-laden branches overhung the road, Roy said, "Turn here."

John Paine and Jimmy Martins involuntarily slowed their steps. They had to be prodded along by the guns in their backs.

Presently, leaves rustled behind the men. It was Judy in the distance, following. When she caught up, all five walked deeper into the woods.

They threaded their way between trees and overgrown roots that lay thick and twisting upon the ground. The soil was still soft from last night's rain. Gradually, the sound of rushing water became audible in the distance.

"Stop here," Roy said.

John and Jimmy halted so abruptly it seemed to the others as if an unseen hand had reached out of the sky to smack them.

John cleared his throat. "Now what?"

Roy held his eyes. "Turn around. Both of you."

Jimmy Martins started to cry.

John Paine looked up at the sky. He looked to the twining trees, the glinting sun, to God Almighty who wasn't going to let him see his baby born. Why? he asked silently.

"Strip," Roy ordered. "Hal, Judy, get their clothes."

Jimmy half turned. "Please!" He scrubbed at his

tear-streaked face, appearing as if at any moment he would beg.

"We can do this quick or slow," Roy answered.

Jimmy dropped his head and turned back around. He raised his hands to his jacket and slowly unzipped it. He glanced once at John, who didn't look back. The older man just kept his eyes on the sky, then he started to unzip.

Finally, when both men were nearly down to skin, Roy gestured with his gun at their briefs. "Those, too."

John shook his head. His briefs came off. Jimmy's followed while his crying turned to loud sobs.

Suddenly without warning, Hal rushed up to Jimmy, jammed his gun behind his ear, and pulled the trigger.

Involuntarily, John Paine stumbled backward, holding his arms in front of his face. "Jesus! Help me!"

Hal swung the gun to him and pulled the trigger again.

Breathing hard, his eyes a little wild, Hal stared down at the dead men. He lowered his gun and turned to look at Roy. Judy, who was standing a little behind Hal, looked at Roy, too.

Roy turned his own gun back inside his pocket and watched the other man. Hal's mouth opened and closed, opened and closed without a word. Roy thought he looked like a fish. Irritated, he snapped, "Get the tools. Judy, bring their clothes over here."

Hal dropped the bag to the ground and hunkered down to unzip it. Judy, the dead men's clothes in her arms, walked over to help.

Roy joined them and took one of the two shovels they pulled from the bag. Hal hefted out the other. The two men stood up and looked around, agreed on a spot to their right, and started to dig.

Less than thirty minutes later, the shallow grave was almost invisible, covered as it was by an abundant smattering of dirt, sticks, and leaves. One or two days of wind, sun, more falling leaves and, if they were lucky, more rain, would make the obscurity complete.

The burial done, Roy and Hal started stripping out of their own clothes. Except for the underwear, they began to don the dead men's uniforms. They'd gauged their victims' physical similarities carefully. The fit of their clothes was nearly perfect.

Judy, having stored the shovels back inside the oilskin sack, sat down on a tree stump to dispassionately watch the show.

When the men were finished, she handed the bag back to Hal and took an armful of their clothes. Roy carried those she couldn't. All three started back out of the woods to the road.

At the front of the truck, Roy handed off his bundle to Judy. She and Hal picked their way down the ravine to the Buick. Short minutes later when they were back, Judy announced, "It's all in the trunk."

Roy gestured toward the delivery truck and said to her, "You get in the back. We'll let you out when we're close enough, then come for the car after."

"Okay." Judy waited for Hal to climb into the cab to pull the keys from the ignition, then she followed him and Roy around the rear of the truck. The fourth key Hal tried was the right one, and he unlocked the door and pushed it up to let her inside.

Judy looked around, taking in a plush easy chair and sofa, both covered with plastic, and other pieces of expensive looking furniture. She sat down on the chair.

Hal joined Roy back up in the cab of the truck.

"Nine o'clock, doing good," Roy announced. He threw the transmission into gear. "Lattimore's been called by now. He knows the delivery's running late."

They traveled less than two miles down the still empty road before turning south and continuing, slowly now, down a section lined with bushes and trees. Behind the trees was the twelve-foot black iron fence that surrounded Paul Lattimore's property.

At the baby pines they'd scouted out a week ago, Roy stopped the truck. Hal trotted around to the back to help Judy out. She moved behind the pines and adjacent bushes while Hal got back inside. Roy kept driving south.

At the end of the road was a deserted four-way stop that bordered the west side of the property. Nothing coming. Roy turned left. They were at the front of the estate now and sighted, not two feet in front of them, the black mailbox that bore Lattimore's white-numeraled address on its black steel post.

Beside the box were the massive gate doors. Right inside them, off the narrow drive that snaked away into the trees that bordered the drive, was the guard's shelter. The guard spotted them and got up to unlock the gate.

Roy mouthed to Hal, "Like clockwork."

Judy heard Charles Lattimore before she actually saw him. Cute little boy. Blond. Big green eyes, just like in his pictures. A little small for his age, but that would only help keep things manageable.

His hands were shoved inside his jacket pockets and he kept looking over his shoulder. She wondered what lie he'd told in order to get past his father and the guard at the front gate?

Whatever, she had faith it was a good one. If nothing else, she'd learned from their clandestine conversations that he was a smart little boy.

And willful. Fortunately, she'd done her job well. His willfullness was an invaluable aid to the cause, combined with his determination. And she'd made sure he was feeling determined about the meeting.

Charlie Lattimore was bent on seeing the ghost he thought waited for him.

Judy watched him come closer like a little lamb to the slaughter.

She tightened the belt of her blue cotton coat and raised the hood over the ball cap she'd donned, partially obscuring the features of her face.

He'd told Dick he'd be back in fifteen minutes. Charlie still expected the security guard to walk up on him any minute. Dick respected Charlie's privacy because Dick knew about Charlie's little trips to the gazebo, including those he wanted to keep secret from his father. But Dick also worried about him, just like his father.

Charlie watched his feet, thinking his father did that a lot lately—worry—even though he tried to respect his son's requests for time alone.

Charlie couldn't tell his father his moodiness was because of his confusion abut *her* calls to their city house. Once, Charlie had almost told until he remembered how sad and depressed his dad had been after his mother had died. Then, his father had cried late at night after he thought Charlie was asleep.

Charlie didn't ever want to see his father cry like that again, and he knew telling him about the calls would make him cry. It would be even worse if he explained to his father how the woman calling herself his mother kept telling him his father had lied to him. She kept telling Charlie his father deliberately hadn't let him come to the hospital, where she'd supposedly died. He'd just seen that big black coffin at the cemetery that could have had anybody in it.

The story about her death had all been a trick, she said, to take Charlie away from her because his dad hadn't loved her anymore.

"That's why I come to you in dreams, my darling," she told him, "because deep down in your heart, you know the truth." Charlie looked over his shoulder again.

Even as he let her talk each time she called, Charlie continued to believe his father had told him the *real* truth. He and his father were a team. His father had helped him past the bad time, when she'd passed away. That meant Charlie now had to help his father by protecting him.

Whoever *she* was, he'd tell his father all about her and the things she said only after he knew more about her, starting today . . .

"Mama!" He stopped walking, telling himself he

couldn't be seeing what he was seeing by the fence. He took a hesitant step, then another.

She was wearing his mother's coat and hat—the silly blue one they'd chosen at some discount store together. But—his father *hadn't* lied.

"Charlie, honey." She held out her arms, inviting him into her embrace. "Come to Mama, baby."

"You aren't *real!*" Charlie whispered. And suddenly he was afraid. Suddenly, it occurred to him he should have been afraid all along.

Judy's arms slowly dropped. "Don't I look real to you? I even wore this," she gestured at the hat, "because I thought it would make you happy. They've all lied to you, Charlie. You know how your father used to yell at me. You know how he hated me."

"No!"

"Why do you think they kept you away from the hospital? He wanted to make you think I'd stopped loving you when the truth is, he sent me away. But I'm back now. I'll never leave you again." She opened her arms. "Come to me, baby, come on."

Charlie heard the tears in her voice, but he wasn't close enough to actually see them in her eyes. He took another step and another, until he was within arm's reach. Until he could see into her face—see her *eyes*!

Charlie tried to run, but she was too quick, her

hand too fast. The needle came out of nowhere as Charlie felt her other hand muffle his scream.

"Sign for this, please, sir." Roy extended the clip board and the invoice for Paul Lattimore to initial. Hal, waiting by the front door, shifted from one foot to the other. Roy knew how he felt.

Paul Lattimore handed back the board and pen. "Thanks. Bet you guys love days like this for deliveries."

"Sure do." Roy smiled back. "Enjoy your sofa." He met Hal at the door and let Hal push open the screen so that they could walk outside onto the porch, across the lawn, and down the driveway to where the truck was parked.

From beginning to end, the furniture delivery Lattimore had been expecting had taken ten minutes.

Roy started the truck, glanced in the side-view mirror, and saw Paul Lattimore standing in his doorway, still watching. Calmly, he put the truck in gear and they backed down the drive, past the guard's house, past the open iron gates, turned left, then continued down the empty road.

Through their open windows, both men heard the gates electronically clang shut behind them. "Wait," Roy cautioned, when he saw Hal reach for his face. "Wait until we're completely out of sight."

Hal dropped his hand, ignoring the itchy adhesive that held the beard to his skin.

When they arrived at the pines where Judy and the kid should have been, they didn't see anything at first. Then Judy stepped out from behind the cover of the trees to catch their attention.

Roy idled the truck in neutral so that he and Hal could get out to help her.

They both thought Charlie Lattimore looked awfully small, bound, gagged, and huddled on the ground. In fact, Hal thought he looked dead. "He okay?"

"Of course," Judy snapped. "Come on."

Hal gripped Charlie's legs while Judy took his thin shoulders. Roy already had the truck's trailer door partially rolled up for them by the time they got around the back. After Charlie was inside, Judy jumped up behind him. Roy rolled down the doors, temporarily shutting her in to watch the kid.

At the wheel, he headed back to Judy's Buick where they'd make the transfer, and the real show would begin.

Charlie, fading in and out of consciousness, gasped behind the stiff rag that pressed his lips painfully against his teeth. The rag was bad, but his panic made it even worse, harder to breath. "Umm," he groaned behind the cloth, trying to move.

"Keep still, kid, we're almost there." Again, Charlie tried to sit up, but his body felt so heavy he could barely move. He wanted to get a better look at her, to see if she really looked as much like his mother as he'd thought. And he wanted to see what else was inside this darkness.

But he couldn't keep his eyes open. He thought of his father's constant warnings about people who might want to hurt them because of who they were.

And just before the internal darkness closed in again, he thought of nightmares that really did come true to swallow careless little boys like him. *Daddy, I'm sorry.*

Roy and Hal waited for Judy to get the Buick back up the embankment. Once, a small two-door Ford drove past. A little girl's face was plastered against its back window.

Both men unzipped their pants as she watched and partially turned their backs, feigning attendance to nature's call. The little girl pointed and laughed before an adult arm shot from the front of the car and gently hooked her around the neck. She faced forward again as the car accelerated and disappeared out of sight.

A few seconds later, Judy's car emerged. It eased up the incline until it was back on the road, just in front of the truck. She got out, opened the trunk, and took their clothes out.

Roy said, "Why don't you change into your own stuff, and we'll get out of these coveralls back at the truck. We'll get the kid in there when we're through."

Judy agreed.

The men waited for her to scoot inside the car before they walked back to the truck.

It took them no time to strip out of the murdered men's coveralls and into their own sweat shirts, jeans, and nylon vests. Roy said, "Here," handing Hal the truck keys. While Hal sifted through the ring for the right one, Roy stepped back a little, slightly behind him.

Hal had the door open when Roy's arm wrapped around his neck, causing him to stumble. Roy absorbed Hal's weight, pressed his pistol to his temple, and whispered against his ear, "Not a sound or I'll kill you."

"What?" Hal stuttered.

"Shut up." Roy tugged him over until Hal was forced to inch his head around the edge of the truck. They both watched Judy, now standing beside the car, looking down at her feet.

"Hey, you through?" Roy called out. "Something's wrong with the kid. We need help back here."

"What?" Judy started toward them. "He should be out like a light."

"Maybe something's wrong with that sedative you gave him." Roy squeezed Hal's neck when he sensed Hal was about to say something. When Judy was close, Roy pushed Hal and followed him around the truck.

Judy stopped cold when she saw the two men. "What the hell—?"

Roy held Judy's eyes, held the gun to Hal's chest—and pulled the trigger.

"Jesus!" Judy shook her head and started backing away.

Roy shoved Hal against the truck, holding the dying man's limp body steady with his own. Then he looked back at Judy.

"No!"

Roy pointed the pistol at her and fired again.

The slug slammed into her back, taking her breath. In slow motion, she fell to her knees, then facedown onto the road. The cement was cold against her cheek and her eyes stayed open while the sun glared hotly down on her. She couldn't speak, couldn't move.

Then she felt hands close around her ankles. She tried to move her own hands, to claw at the ground, to gain purchase while Roy dragged her painfully back toward the truck. Her face, scraped and bleeding, throbbed like her back as she felt her legs suddenly lifted into the air and placed upon the truck bed. For moments, she hung suspended, then the rest of her was lifted and shoved inside.

Rough cloth—the dead men's clothes—touched her chest. She realized Hal's dead body was pressing against her own. And she saw, just before she lost consciousness, Charlie Lattimore lying still on the ground beside Roy's feet.

For the first time, Roy started to sweat. If somebody came along now . . . A stopped delivery truck along the side of the road only looked inconspicuous if a four-door Buick wasn't three feet away, parked with it. He scooped Charlie up in his arms and ran to the car. His gun bounced against his hip.

The car keys dangled in the ignition where Judy had left them. Roy grabbed them through the open window and turned to the rear door. He opened the door and laid Charlie on the floor behind the front seat.

At the trunk, he removed a gasoline can he'd secretly filled to stash away, along with the oilskin bag of shovels Hal and Judy had watched him carry from her house. Then he hurried back to the rear of the truck, where he started splashing gasoline inside.

Back inside the cab, he started the engine and

moved off the side of the road. Slowly, he eased down the same shallow embankment Judy had used.

The truck was too tall, of course, to achieve the total cover Judy had managed for the Buick. But Roy was able to get it into the bushes and trees until a good portion of it was wedged out of clear sight from the road.

He still didn't see or hear anybody coming and began splashing gasoline around the inside of the cab. Then he pulled a packet of matches from his breast pocket, lit one, and tossed it inside the open driver's window. The whoosh of flames was immediate and intense. He was at the back of the truck with another unlit match when something made him jerk his head around to the road.

A car? *Now?* He looked at Judy and Hal's prone bodies, then back at the road. Couldn't take the chance. He had to get out of here.

With all that gasoline, he thought as he ran back to the Buick, surely it wouldn't take long for the entire truck to ignite. Then it would take only a little longer after that for somebody to investigate, by which time the most critical identifying evidence would be sufficiently damaged.

Roy had no illusions. This fiery rouse ultimately wouldn't save him. But he wasn't looking for failsafe. He was looking for time, and that's what all of this was going to buy him.

With the empty can in his hand, he ran back up the incline to the car. And saw nothing. Maybe there *was* no one. Maybe his nerves were getting to him, and maybe there was still time to go back, light the inside after all . . .

Fuck it. He threw himself inside the Buick and twisted the key in the ignition. If his life had taught him anything, it was that luck never held. He gunned the accelerator and sped down the empty road.

The smoke roused her. Judy opened her eyes and coughed, realizing immediately what was happening. Her throat felt scorched from the overpowering fumes of gasoline and smoke.

She made it to her knees and crawled to the edge of the truck. Her back was a mass of agony. Her breath was labored, but she propelled herself forward through the flames, fell, and hit the ground hard.

She breathed in the scent of dead, cold leaves, felt soft moist dirt against her mouth. The heat from the truck was intense and terrifying. Fire and black smoke billowed from the front and down along the sides of the truck to where the wind blew it, to where she tried to stand.

With a superhuman effort, she did stand and made it over to a tree. She clutched the knobby trunk just as she heard something. Traffic? Behind her. Up the incline.

She pushed away from the tree and made it up the rise just as everything inside her mind went dark again.

It was ten-oh-five a.m.

Chapter Two

"Okay, you guys, let's move it, we're losing her!" The young Morgan County General paramedic gripped the top of the stretcher while one of his two colleagues took the opposite end and the third shoved open the ambulance door. Burn victims were always bad, the first paramedic thought. But this poor woman. Damn, she probably wouldn't survive the night.

At the hospital, the three were met by the resident in charge of the emergency ward. "What have we got?" she demanded, trotting just ahead of them to a treatment room.

"Gunshot wound to the back," one of the paramedics answered. "Third-degree burns, lacerations, and head trauma, and shock."

"Jesus. Where did you find her?"

The paramedic turned his head slightly, gesturing in back of him to a man and woman who stood down the hallway. Concerned, horrified looks were etched into their faces. "They found her at the side of some ditch off a state road two miles from here. Called it in to the state police."

The doctor looked back at the couple just before she pulled the curtain to the treatment room closed. "So why are they still here?"

The paramedic shrugged. "Said they didn't want to leave until they knew if she makes it."

The doctor looked down at the woman whose face, arms, and upper torso were disfigured with mud, blood, and burned skin. She murmured, "Well, they may not have to wait long."

Indianapolis
Two p.m.

Sean Alexander shouldered the front door to his condo closed, shutting out the brisk fall air, fragrant with a neighbor's burning leaves. Three months ago, he had been an FBI special agent-in-charge, trusted with supervising an Indianapolis field office of men and women through sensitive federal investigations.

The only thing he was in charge of this afternoon was getting out of the damp, sleek insulated running gear he wore. After that, he would cool down with a mug of hot strong coffee. He supposed for the thousandth time he should have felt guilty about his static leisure.

Instead, he was disquieted that the most he still felt was relief.

He walked straight to the kitchen, unzipping his jacket as he went. He stripped it off, casually tossing it on a dining room chair. The T-shirt he wore underneath was adequate inside the coziness of his condo.

In the kitchen, he reached between a set of canisters on the counter to flick on a small portable radio. Details of the latest-breaking national headline news from the public radio station he kept tuned droned in companionable counterpoint to the quiet.

From a cabinet over the sink he pulled down a package of the specially ground coffee blend he preferred—sent to him by his aunt Moira all the way from Dublin, bless her. He was anticipating its rich bite, pouring water into his coffee machine, when fragments of something the newscaster was saying caught his attention.

"*. . . Though details are sketchy at the moment, the FBI has confirmed that a local search is underway. Lattimore is assisting the authorities. The president . . .*"

The wall phone behind him shrilled. Sean watched it for a moment, an uneasy prickling along the back of his neck, then he picked it up.

"Alexander."

"You've heard?"

FBI Deputy Director Devlin Thompson listened for an answer, Sean knew, all the way from Washington, D.C. And Sean could tell by Thompson's clipped tone that the deputy director wasn't asking just now as a friend. "About Lattimore?" Sean waited for the clarification he suddenly knew he didn't want to hear.

"Yeah, it's his boy. Charlie Lattimore disappeared this morning. It's a kidnapping, Sean, there's no doubt."

Sean felt the faint chill that had followed him inside the house solidify into something still and cold. "Dev, you know I'm still out of this. Why are you calling me now?"

"Why the hell do you think? It's been three months since you requested a leave of absence, Sean. How long does it take?"

How long *should* it take, Sean heard. "Parker is acting SAC. He's fully capable—"

"The president himself has intervened on this one. Lattimore is more than just a retired senator. You know how the president is when it comes to supporting his close personal friends."

Sean stared at the coffee dripping steadily into the carafe in front of him. When Thompson spoke again, Sean heard his concern. And his pity. He hated them.

"There was blood at the scene, Sean."

Goddammit, Sean thought.

"Nobody wants to suspect the worst this soon, but—"

Sean waited.

"There's another reason why I think you, specifically, need to be involved in this."

Sean still said nothing.

"Let's talk. I can be out there in three hours."

Feeling trapped, Sean could visualize the noose tightening. "I'm only agreeing to listen."

Thompson sighed.

But Sean thought he sounded relieved.

FBI Headquarters
Washington, D.C.

FBI Director Anthony Collins studied the woman before him. Despite Thompson's argument, he didn't doubt he'd made the right choice.

Special Agent Jennifer Bennett was young, exceptionally talented, and above all ambitious. If by some stroke of luck—bad, in his opinion—Thompson successfully convinced Alexander to come back, Bennett would be right behind him to spare the bureau a fuck-up.

"The truth is simply this," he told her, "I can't trust that he's the man he was before he requested the transfer out of California. Without that assurance, I can't sufficiently trust he's the man for this case."

Jennifer Bennett studied the director and considered her response. He was, with that admission, being wildly indiscreet. And intriguing.

His antagonism against Sean Alexander was no secret within the bureau.

It also was no secret that his feelings had originated three years ago, coinciding with Special Agent Sean Alexander's task force findings of—if not downright discrimination—lethargic promotion of female agents within the bureau. Collins's private displeasure with that embarrassment had been fueled by the public opinion and subsequent political support that had helped guide Alexander to a well-deserved SAC promotion.

Alexander's exceptional performance within that position ever since had chafed Collins like a low-level burn. It was rumored the director's agitation lay mostly in his resentment toward the young agent's effrontery in showing him up.

Of course, Jennifer thought, it was also no secret within the bureau that Director Collins's friendship with her grandfather was a long one. Which probably had something to do with her sitting here now.

The two men's friendship, in fact, had spurred more than a few whispers of favoritism about Bennett's granddaughter, when the ex-Marine had been accepted five years ago into the FBI Academy at Quantico. Even as her abilities were recognized throughout basic training and into her field work, Jennifer's classmates' gentle razzing had been constant.

Nevertheless, it was fact that now at the age of thirty, Jennifer Bennett had set a bureau record for making the fastest grade advancement any agent had ever made within such a young career.

And she knew, even if others wondered, that Gerard Bennett had not reared his granddaughter to expect favors, let alone depend upon them. Jennifer thoroughly believed that in a tough world, incurring favors was just another way of stringing potential rope around your neck when the going got rough for the one you owed. As it inevitably did.

Thus, her suspicion of the favorable break the director was offering her now caused her to respond with caution. "With all due respect, sir, Agent Alexander's ten years with the bureau establish a credibility of their own. No other field operative has achieved as many successful case resolutions as he. Or gained more positive visibility for the bureau."

The director's eyes narrowed.

Jennifer read his reaction as point taken. At his silence, she continued. "No other agent maintains as much professional respect inside the bureau, or popularity outside it as Alexander."

"Yes, the media certainly loved dwelling on that particular stellar moment in his career. The very fiasco that continues to keep him out of commission."

Inwardly, Jennifer agreed. Outwardly, respect for a senior colleague caused her to say, "We both know that scenario could have gone south for any agent. It's everyone's worst collective nightmare. It's also the sort of ultimate price any of us may have to pay for what we do."

"If that's all it is in Alexander's case, why is he still sitting at home? His post-psychological evaluations indicate he should be fit and ready to put California behind him."

Jennifer watched him, thinking *no* agent worth his or her salt could ever entirely put something like that behind them.

"Instead, we sit here having this conversation when you and I both know an agent like you is much more suited to head this case."

Not *like* me, Jennifer heard him say. *Me.* "Why?" she asked bluntly. She wanted to know where this abrupt support was coming from.

Though she'd heard much from her grandfather about the man even before she'd joined the FBI, Collins had never sought a private audience with her. In fact, she'd barely laid eyes on him before now.

Collins shrugged, leaned back in his leather chair,

and crossed his legs as he contemplated his paper-strewn desk. "I owe your grandfather."

Jennifer waited.

"Gerry saved my life in Korea. I told him then nothing he'd ever ask of me would be too great a favor to grant. He wants the best for his granddaughter. Since you've chosen the bureau as the proving ground for your talents, I'm in a position to make his wish come true. Fortunately, this Lattimore development allows me to merge his wishes with mine."

Jennifer tried to focus on the professional compliment instead of the slight insult. As for her grandfather's well-intentioned meddling, she'd deal with him later. Collins leaned forward, folding his hands in front of him.

"The truth is, Jennifer, we need a victory. This bureau should never have been put into the positions, either accidental or self-perpetuated, that have caused it to take the hits it's sustained. It's all because of indecision at the highest levels of leadership, because of softness creeping in where there used to be strength."

Jennifer made the connection Collins clearly wanted her to make to Sean Alexander.

"The low opinion the public has of us is unprecedented and unacceptable. It never happened in Hoover's days. For all his flaws, he understood the importance of perception and made sure some things were done right. Now I'm committed to doing everything I can to restore the bureau's reputation. That means I need the brightest and the best at the forefront of my watch."

"Sir—"

"Nobody disputes that Alexander is a good man, a dedicated one. But right now, he's also a wounded one and this kidnapping's resolution can't afford that sort of hindrance at the outset."

"Sir, I'm betting Lattimore is already prepared to go to the media with emotional appeals to the kidnapper or kidnappers, *and* with attention grabbing ones to Alexander, the media's pet, if we don't convince Alexander to take control of this situation first."

Collins reached inside his breast pocket for a pack of cigarettes. From across his desk, he pulled an ashtray that had sat empty on doctor's orders for nearly a year. "I'm aware of that. That's why what I propose is this." He paused to light his cigarette.

"When we release the controlled details of this kidnapping to the media in," he checked his watch, "less than thirty minutes, it's going to grab the heart of the nation. The people of this country loved Paul Lattimore as a senator. They still love him as a state congressman. If it's Alexander he wants, it's Alexander he'll have, provided Alexander agrees."

Collins rose from his chair to walk to the window

behind his desk. His back to Jennifer, he continued. "What I want is some insurance against him. That's where you come in."

"What kind of insurance?"

"I want you to watch Alexander's back. If he's functional, fine. If he's not, you're going to be there to push him aside and clean up the mess."

Jennifer was beyond wincing at the director's bluntness. Many agents called him crude and insensitive. His organizational record judged him brutally efficient. For her own part, Jennifer had learned at the academy that liking a superior's personality didn't necessarily need to be a prerequisite for respecting his abilities.

Whatever else she felt about Collins, she had no reason to question his professional judgement.

"Tell me the truth, Director Collins. My grandfather aside, why am I here?" Jennifer thought it only prudent to get him to say flat out what he really expected of her.

Collins hesitated then said, "Ever since your days in the academy, I've known you were going places. Your instructors thought so. Many of your classmates did, too. They still do. Yes," he smiled slightly at her raised brow, "I've been keeping tabs. Inevitable, I'd say, considering you're Gerry Bennett's grandchild. But that aside, your field performance has played out that promise. I want leaders like you. The bureau needs agents who aren't afraid to be aggressive, and political correctness be damned.''

It also wouldn't hurt your reputation that such an agent be a woman, Jennifer thought cynically. But more pressing was Collins's additional not-so-veiled jab at Sean Alexander. In fact, she needed to take a moment to figure out how she felt about where he was coming from on that.

Because after all, hadn't she become, at least within bureau ranks, one of Alexander's most vocal detractors for much the same reasoning Collins was expressing?

Collins turned away from the window to face her. "Don't get me wrong. I have as much appreciation for Alexander as anyone in this bureau. But the time inevitably comes when even the most formidable warriors get battle weary and have to step down.''

Looking into Collins's flinty gray eyes, hearing him echo the concerns about Alexander's apparent burnout she shared, Jennifer knew what her answer to his unorthodox request would be. Putting aside her personal admiration for Sean Alexander's past achievements, she'd felt strongly for some time that the agent had seemingly met the foe he couldn't defeat—one of the mind.

For a field agent charged with the command of dedicated men and women, that struggle would eventually turn fatal.

Jennifer stood up. "How soon may I leave for Indiana sir?"

"You're already booked on a flight that's out of here in ninety minutes." He reached inside his breast pocket and handed her a ticket. "Don't let me down."

After a moment, Jennifer stepped forward to accept the ticket. She nodded, then turned to leave the office. As she closed the door behind her, she acknowledged the secretary who looked up from her computer screen with a polite smile.

Jennifer hit the elevator button in the hallway. Collins was mistaken. She didn't owe whatever was going to transpire to him, or even to her grandfather. Collins had admonished her not to let him down. He was, of course, at liberty to believe whatever he wanted about the motivation that shaped her loyalties.

But what she would ensure he and everyone else came to understand was that Jennifer Bennett's allegiance wasn't to Anthony Collins. It was and always would be to the bureau both she and he had taken an oath of fidelity, bravery, and integrity to serve.

Sean's hand tightened around his beer when he heard the knock on the front door. He glanced at the clock on the fireplace mantle. Five o'clock. He set the can down beside the clock and walked out of the study into a narrow foyer to let his friend in.

He could see Dev's tall, rangy silhouette through the mullioned glass before he swung open the door. Devlin Thompson, five years his senior at a fit forty-one, didn't look happy to see him. Aside from the obvious reason why, Sean understood and stepped aside, letting Thompson in.

Thompson followed him through the short hallway into the spare, neat study Sean had just left. Sean watched Thompson, thinking that Dev must be remembering the times he'd been here in happier days. Sean didn't miss the way his friend's eyes went to the can on the mantle before he took the sofa Sean had vacated and settled that shrewd gaze on him.

"You don't have a choice, Sean," he said, coming straight to the point. "You know that."

Sean meandered back to the fireplace, where he reclaimed his beer.

Thompson's smile was humorless. "That won't work, you know. Maybe you can bullshit some others, but not me. We've known each other too long."

Sean faced Thompson and emptied the can, keeping his eyes on the older man's. Still not saying anything, he set the can back down, turned to face the flames, and rested his weight on his outstretched arms along the mantle. "That's precisely why you shouldn't have come. I'm not ready."

"Whatever else you've portrayed yourself as, I never would have expected this self-pity."

Sean shrugged. "Aren't you listening? What did I just tell you?"

Thompson pushed himself to his feet. "Goddammit, then. Maybe you're right."

Sean swung around. "Dev, wait—"

Thompson kept walking.

"Dammit. I said stop."

"Give me a good reason to."

Sean sighed heavily. "Because I can be a real son-of-a-bitch. You know that about me, too."

Thompson wavered.

Sean waited, honestly not knowing what Thompson would do, until he finally walked back to the sofa and sat down.

Sean took the opposite end, folding his hands over an upraised knee. "Tell me, then."

"Lattimore called Collins directly to report the kidnapping."

"Why is he sure it's a kidnapping? The boy didn't just take off?"

"There was a note and a ransom request for ten million dollars."

"He was snatched from where?"

"Lattimore's farmhouse, a few miles south of here. Lattimore built it as a retreat where he could get away from the city. The property belonged to his

41

wife, and he's continued to go there each year since she died."

Sean thought about that. He knew Devlin Thompson, too, was thinking it ironic that Sean, one of those former friends, hadn't known these recent details about Paul. Sean was also remembering the cloying press Paul Lattimore had endured when his wife had tragically been diagnosed with the cancer that had killed her. Now this with his son. He looked back into the fire.

"Listen, Sean. Paul won't take no for an answer. In fact, Collins confided to me that he actually asked the president to use his influence with you if it came to that. Everyone knows you can't be forced to do this, but Paul is asking."

Sean kept watching the flames.

"I know you don't want to hear it, but I'm going to say it again. Paul respects you, respects what you've built a reputation doing better than many other agents in the bureau. When a situation is at its tightest, there's nobody who's proven he's better to have in the good guys' corner than you. Despite everything, Paul still knows that. I think, deep down, you still know it, too."

"Doesn't he read the papers?"

"When are you going to stop crucifying yourself?"

Sean got up restlessly. At the hearth, he reached for an andiron and poked at the logs. The dying embers sparked, struggled, then caught again. "Has a team been put together?"

"We're doing it now. Come with me to the crime scene. Make an evaluation before you give me your answer."

Sean looked over his shoulder at Thompson.

"Just trust me." Thompson sighed. "I'll be honest. While Lattimore wants you, there are others in the bureau, maybe some you'd be working with, who don't. Not because of what happened," he added, seeing the flicker in Sean's eyes, "because of what they think it's done to you."

Sean turned back to the flames. "Maybe they're right."

"If I believed that, I wouldn't be here. You know me well enough to believe me when I tell you I'm saying that not as your friend, but as your superior."

Keeping his back to Thompson, Sean asked, "How old is Charlie now?"

"Only ten."

A log shifted. Sparks flared. "You said there was blood." Sean turned to face Thompson. "Is his kid alive, Dev?"

Thompson hesitated.

Sean waited.

"Like I said, come with me. You'll have the answers to some of these questions after you see things for yourself."

Now Sean hesitated, pondering the ball that had been tossed back into his court.

"Dammit, Sean, we're wasting time you know that kid doesn't have!"

Sean sighed bitterly. Duty warred with resentment. He was already guessing which would win.

Thompson offered to drive, arguing that he was familiar enough with Lattimore's property and the territory surrounding it to save time by taking the wheel himself.

Sean let him. He used the reprieve to sit on the passenger side, quiet with his thoughts. In fact, now that they were on their way, neither man said much. Until they got there, there really wasn't much to say.

Thompson navigated the interstate that circled the city with competent speed. From his own side window, Sean watched the panorama of commercial complexes, apartment communities, and long stretches of open field roll by.

When he narrowed his eyes, the vista appeared to be an unending ocean of wild browning grass. When he closed them completely, the grass disappeared, replaced by a vision of another ocean, one that was real and blue and endless. One that still haunted his dreams.

The elementary school sat on top of the hill, miles from the distant water. It overlooked the sleepy, up-

scale Southern California community that embraced
it. The day was edging into late morning, the sifting
ocean air a balm to the coast and to the young afflu-
ent families who, seduced, flocked to it.

A fragrant breeze gently cooled and caressed
Sean's face, but it barely penetrated the flack jackets
he and his men wore. The terrorist inside the schoolhouse was on the verge of coming out of the building
after the third day of the standoff.

The terrorist's two cohorts were likewise on the
verge of surrendering the children they held—releasing them to the safekeeping of the federal agents,
hostage recovery specialists, family, and media who
stood tensely assembled to receive them. Then . . .
without warning, the world went from blindingly
bright to blindingly black. A collective scream from
the onlookers mingled with the explosions inside
the school.

Panic. Chaos. Desolation. Death . . .

"Sean, for God's sake, wake *up*."

Sean roused under Dev's jostling hand. Slowly, he
pulled back from the nightmare, back into the reality
of the autumn-colored world outside the car and the
crisis that was relentlessly drawing him back where
he didn't want to go. He sat up, scrubbing a hand
across his jaw.

Thompson was subdued. "If that's what you're
living with, no wonder—"

"I'm handling it."

"It occurs to me you should be handling it better by now. I thought the bureau—"

"I said I'm handling it, Dev. Drop it."

A moment of tense silence stretched between them, then Thompson turned his full attention back to the road.

They exited onto the southbound state road that, forty minutes later, emptied them into the rural community where the abduction had occurred. Thompson slowed along a narrow backroad until he turned onto another that led into Lattimore's property.

A half dozen cars Sean recognized as bureau were clustered in front of a rambling three-story brick farmhouse. Among them was a sheriff's squad car, beside which stood a heavy-set uniformed man Sean assumed was the sheriff. He was deep in conversation with two FBI agents. A crime scene vehicle sat off to the right against the side of the front drive that disappeared around the house.

Several yards from the house, a section outside the gate just bordering the woods was cordoned off with yellow tape to make the actual crime scene location. Uniformed local cops and one more agent were talking there with Lattimore. Even from this distance, Sean could see how shaken Paul Lattimore was.

"Come on." Thompson opened his door and got out. Sean followed in Lattimore's direction. He glanced back at the security gates, thinking how ironic it was that just a few hours ago the imposing iron would have seemed incongruous against Lattimore's unassuming house.

As they trudged through the soft fallen leaves, Sean nodded to the agents. They weren't entirely successful hiding expressions of surprise as he passed by.

Then Lattimore looked up. He broke away from the agent questioning him and, meeting the two men, gripped Sean's hand.

"Sean, thank God!"

"Paul, I'm sorry."

"You've got to catch—my little boy's only ten." His eyes, already red, started tearing again. "Jesus *Christ*."

Sean squeezed his shoulder. In the face of a parent's anguish there was never anything adequate to say.

"Paul, we'll talk in a moment," Thompson said. "First, I need Sean to see this."

If possible, the expression in Lattimore's eyes turned even more distressed. "Sure. I'll be right here." He jammed his hands inside his coat pockets and gazed down at the ground, as if searching for answers he desperately needed.

Sean followed Thompson to where the agent Lattimore had been talking to stood alone. All that registered with Sean in that brief glance was that the agent was a woman and that she was tall, slim, and black.

And then his attention was moving over to the patch of ground just outside an unlocked opening in the fence. He stood riveted, working through surprise, then anger.

At his feet, buried half in and half out of the soil, was a child's teddy bear. It was matted with large splotches of blood. The possible symbolism of the stains jolted him.

Suddenly conscious of the fact that Lattimore had joined them, Sean demanded, "Is this Charlie's?" Even to his own ears, his voice sounded raw.

"No. He hasn't owned one since he was a baby. You know how it is now, Nintendo and all those other computer games."

After a moment, Thompson said, "Do you understand now why you needed to see this, Sean?"

Lattimore glanced between the two men. "What's going on?"

"Maybe a message," Sean said and abruptly turned away. He walked down the line of trees, away from the crime scene, the other agents, the local cops. That goddamned bear.

"Agent Alexander?"

Sean turned to the female agent who had broken away from the other two to follow him. She was beautiful, he thought for a disconcerted moment. Stunning, actually.

Light brown skin, narrow, delicate features that softly emphasized a full, sensuous mouth. Thick medium-length black hair pulled neatly back into a gold clip at her nape. The severity of it dramatically tempered by delicate wisps that escaped the confinement to flirt with the smooth line of her jaw and ears. An additional curling fringe resting bluntly over deeply lashed almond-shaped brown eyes.

Then he realized the concern in those eyes was mixed with something else. Something not so benevolent.

She held out her hand. "I'm Special Agent Jennifer Bennett. I understand we'll be working together on this one."

Jennifer Bennett. He didn't know her, but something about the name niggled. It worried him for a moment, then he let it go. "Your understanding may be premature."

Jennifer Bennett, who had been holding his dark gaze with hers, must have heard something terse enough in his answer to make her take that involuntary step back, he observed.

"Agent Bennett, would you leave us alone for a moment?" Thompson had silently arrived unnoticed by either of them. Sean caught a glint of impatience in Bennett's expression, but she murmured, "Sure," and walked back over to the crime scene. Sean turned to Thompson.

"So," Thompson said. "What are you going to do?"

Sean looked at his superior, heard concern from his friend, felt his last hope of escape slipping away. Inexplicably, he thought of Jennifer Bennett, and a small piece of memory clicked into place. "She's out of Washington, isn't she?"

Thompson looked at him.

"I see. Sent all the way up here, was she?"

Thompson still didn't answer.

"Why, Dev?" Justifiable suspicion or occupational paranoia? Experience had taught Sean that this business often mandated it healthy to consider them one and the same. "On second thought, I don't even want to hear it. I have a feeling I'll find out soon enough."

"Sean—"

"Just tell me this. How could she have been informed already that we'd be 'working together?' Either you or Collins made one hell of a presumption."

"No, I was betting on the truest professional I've ever known. And looking into your eyes now, I'd say my bet's still good."

Sean looked away from Thompson, back over at the yellow tape. His eyes touched the slender back of Special Agent Jennifer Bennett, then moved on to Lattimore. Gone was the unflappable Capitol Hill senator perpetually in control, notoriously so when in front of the nastiest media sharks and their cameras. In his place stood an ordinary frightened man, humbled by a father's worst fear, quietly swiping at the tears that wetted his face. Poignantly reminiscent of a child as young as the one he was missing.

Only ten, Sean thought.

"Damn you, Dev. Damn you all." He looked up at the cloud-spattered sky, took a deep breath, then slowly exhaled.

Chapter Three

Charlie's tears had abated long ago, but not his terror.

He lay wedged on the backseat floor of the Buick. His bound wrists were numb and he was fighting another of the dozes he kept falling in and out of. He didn't want to sleep so much, but the combined effects of the drug he'd been given and his fear of what this man was going to do to him were dulling his defenses.

The car stopped. Coming awake again, Charlie tried to sit up. The back door was thrown open. A rush of cool air followed the tall man who crawled inside and onto the back seat.

Charlie scooted back against the opposite door. When the man just climbed further inside, Charlie made a frightened sound.

The man raised his hand. Charlie caught himself, but started trembling. The man responded by reaching inside a breast pocket of his vest. He pulled out a wrapped candy bar and extended it. "Here," he said.

Charlie stared at the food as if it would bite.

"Aren't you hungry?"

Charlie looked into the man's eyes, really seeing his face for the first time. To his surprise, he didn't look like a monster. He looked like a geek.

Short blond hair, almost as pale as his clean-shaven skin, hung limply on his small head. His brows, yellow too, slashed across light, unblinking eyes. All at once, Charlie thought the man looked like a snake.

"What are you staring at? I said, aren't you hungry?"

"Are you going to untie me so I can eat?"

The man seemed surprised by his answer. Then he looked thoughtful. "Are you going to give me trouble?"

Charlie considered the question and the man's calculating look. He swallowed. "I'll be good."

The man watched him, as if trying to decide whether or not he could trust him. At last, he reached inside his other breast pocket and withdrew a small knife.

Charlie's eyes grew round again. Again, he tried to scoot back. The man gave him a surprised, kind of hurt look.

"I'm just going to take the rope off," he said. "You want that, don't you?"

Charlie's heart was hammering. "Yes," he whispered, keeping his eyes on the knife.

"Then move back over here and let me. It's okay, you can trust me." He smiled.

Charlie decided he liked the man's looks better when he didn't smile. Cautiously, he did as the man asked. Just as cautiously, the man said, "Now turn around."

Charlie did.

The man moved behind him.

Charlie could smell the odor of stale cigarettes and fainter ones of gasoline and sweat coming off his skin. He made himself hold still when he felt the blade of the knife brush against his bound hands. Three sawing movements later, his wrists were free.

"Ow!" he said involuntarily when needles shot down his arms as he moved them. The man moved away and sat crouched on his knees, watching him.

Charlie looked beyond him, out the open door of the car. He could see there were a bunch of trees and an empty road. Along both sides of the road, dead corn stalks stretched out tall and brown forever. No one to help. No one at all in sight. His eyes snapped forward again when the man spoke.

"Are you listening, kid? I said here's the deal. As long as you promise to stay good, I'll let you ride up front with me. I'm going to stop someplace and get us some real food. But when I do, you're not going to try to get out of the car, because I'll hurt you. Even if I have to run you down to do it, I'll hurt you. Understand me?"

"Yes, sir."

"Because I really don't want to hurt you. Do you believe that?"

"Yes, sir."

The man reached out and ran a caressing hand across Charlie's forehead.

Charlie's skin crawled, but he held still and kept silent.

"I would never hurt you, boy," the man murmured. "You believe that?"

"Yes," Charlie responded. He was rewarded with the man's strangely distant smile. Then the man backed out of the car and held out a hand.

"Come on, get out."

Charlie forced himself to take that hand. It was soft, cold, clammy. But Charlie held on, sensing calm cooperation meant his life. The man, still smiling, led him to the front passenger side of the car. He opened the door and with an encouraging look urged Charlie to scoot inside.

Charlie did and sat there like a stone. Now what? Nothing in sight but endless fields and, in the distance, more trees.

From the other side of the car, the driver's door opened, making Charlie jump. The man got inside and started the engine. "You feel like hamburgers?" he asked almost cheerfully, and put the car in gear.

Charlie nodded. He felt like whatever it was going to take to keep him alive.

"Let's see the note." Sean took the small square of lined paper from a deputy and dropped into one of two easy chairs flanking the unlit fireplace inside Lattimore's living room. Sean and the other agents, the sheriff, and two county deputies were gathered inside Lattimore's house.

Devlin Thompson had already said his farewells to his men and was on his way back to Washington.

And so now the agents and police officers all sat around, aided with mugs of hot coffee provided by Sarah Jennings, Lattimore's seasonal housekeeper, to assemble what pieces to the case they had and to review what they knew. Sean scanned over the message he'd already memorized.

Gotcha! Or I will in five days. I want ten million, in untraceable bills. Delivery point to be announced, so stand by. You want your boy back, remember the luck of the Irish and these words to LIVE by: All good things come to those who wait. So long, for now.

*   *   *

Sheriff Jed Mauer sat with his bulk perched on a sofa across from Sean. From his clipped answers and poker expression, Sean judged he and his men were reserving judgement on the Feds who had descended on their territory. Everybody knew that the rules dictated the federal agency's role was to foster teamwork with local authorities, to assist where necessary and appropriate.

Everyone also knew that in many cases, especially ones as high-profile as this one, local guys were inclined to resentfully think the FBI automatically presumed superiority.

The team of agents assembled for this case were, as it turned out, colleagues Sean knew of but had not actually worked with in the past. They were proven professionals whose records collectively demonstrated their capabilities to him. Except, of course, one.

Jennifer Bennett stood quietly listening within the assembled group. Something in her manner gave her the appearance of standing apart from them. Sean wasn't sure he liked that. Or the way she watched him. He'd have to deal with it soon.

"This is all he left at the crime scene, besides the bear?" Sean threw the question out to everyone. Mauer answered.

"Yeah. But it's pretty clear what he wants, and the

blood on that bear proves he ain't jackin' around here."

"Obviously. Paul," Sean turned to Lattimore, "what else can you tell us?"

Lattimore looked a little startled. "About what, specifically? Beyond what I've told Sheriff Mauer about my last conversation with Charlie this morning, not much."

Sean looked at him closely. He knew Lattimore's mental lethargy was a result of shock, but they didn't have time. "Think harder, Paul. Who could have had a reason to do this? Have you been harassed lately, or received any threatening calls?"

"No."

"None at all?"

"No."

"What about indirectly? Anything you dismissed as ridiculous, or maybe someone you wrote off as a crank?"

"Nothing, Sean."

Jennifer said, "What about anything out of the ordinary from your staff or friends? Did anyone say anything to you before you and Charlie took off for the woods, anything that strikes you now as questionable?"

"I've never made any public secret of the fact that Charlie and I have been coming down here for the past two years since my wife died. Indiana is my home, and the property is almost all I have left of Cheryl.

"If you're asking for anything out of the ordinary in any of that, it's all public knowledge, isn't it? If you're looking for someone who could have done something unusual with that knowledge, you might as well look anywhere in the country."

He was right. Sean watched the knowledge register in Bennett's eyes, only to be overridden by something more urgent. "Mr. Lattimore, sometimes you glean more than you think from a conversation, a casual word, what you'd normally dismiss as something inconsequential. Perhaps that's the case here. Are you sure—"

"Agent Bennett, I've said I can't think of anything. My little boy is gone. Please, I've just got to—" his voice broke.

"It's okay, Paul." Sean glanced at Bennett before he soothingly went on. "Let's go over it again. Everything was quiet around here before Charlie left the house, prior to his abduction? No visitors or phone calls."

"None. Except, of course for the furniture delivery. But that had been set up weeks ago."

They already planned to check out the furniture store. "And that delivery went as arranged, you said."

"Yes, more or less."

Less, Sean thought. They knew about the delivery truck, which had been discovered burning not five miles away earlier in the day. They also knew about the single body, apparently burned beyond recognition, in the back of a vehicle that should have contained two.

Add to that the mystery of the woman who had been discovered a few yards from there, shot, burned, and clearly connected with whatever had gone down with that truck.

"Was there anything odd about the delivery men? Did they act suspicious in any way? Were either of them out of your sight for any length of time?"

Lattimore was already shaking his head. "No. The store called to tell me they were running about twenty minutes or so late on the delivery. But that can't mean anything right? I mean, the *store* called."

Sean nodded reassuringly. His eyes briefly met Jennifer Bennett's. They both knew the circumstances of that call would be thoroughly checked out, too.

"Okay. So after the men made the delivery, then what?"

"About fifteen minutes later, I started getting worried that Charlie hadn't come back from his walk yet."

"That time lapse was unusual?"

"Well, it was since he promised me he'd be back

in about thirty minutes, tops. Charlie doesn't lie, he knows how I worry about him, especially since—"

"Yes?" Sean urged.

Lattimore sighed. "Since Cheryl died. They are," he paused again, "they were everything to me. Now my son's well-being means just that much more. And his happiness."

"And walking the grounds makes Charles happy?"

"He has a special place, just outside the grounds. A gazebo where he and Cheryl used to spend time together during our vacations down here. He thinks I don't know about the visits he sneaks off to make there. But Dick, the security guard, keeps me informed."

"Because he keeps a special eye on Charlie during those times, too."

"Yes."

"And in fact it was Dick who called up to the house to tell you when Charlie appeared to be gone."

"Yes.

"And it was Dick who was with you as you searched the grounds around the house and found the note and teddy bear."

"Yes."

Sean made a note on the pad of paper that rested in his lap. "Who else knew about Charlie's clandestine visits to the gazebo?"

"No one. That is, nobody around here."

"What do you mean around here?" Jennifer said.

Sean glanced at her, then back at Paul, waiting for his answer.

"I mean his therapist, Emily Marsh, knew. The habit was part of Charlie's dependency on his mother's memory. Emily worked hard to wean him away from it after Cheryl died."

"What precisely was she treating Charlie for?"

"Severe depression. It started when Cheryl got sick. It only got worse after she died."

"Did Dr. Marsh know about your planned vacation here at the cabin?"

"Not specifically. She knows I tend to bring Charlie down every fall. But we hadn't communicated specifically about this particular visit."

Sean made another note. "Is your son still undergoing therapy, Paul?"

"Only on an occasional basis, now. In the last three months, Emily has made tremendous progress. Charlie was starting to come out of it, to be his old self again."

"What is it?" Jennifer prompted, seeing his frown.

Paul Lattimore looked at her, his brow still creased. "One thing's been puzzling in light of Charlie's progress. His grades at school have started falling off again, like before, right after my wife's death. Nothing as serious," he added quickly. "But Charlie's a very bright child. For him, even a slight slacking-off is noticeable."

"What does Emily Marsh say about it?" Sean asked.

"She told me not to be alarmed, that no matter how smart kids are they aren't perfect. That Charlie, no matter how precocious he is, is in most ways just an ordinary little boy, and that boys get distracted."

"But you're thinking maybe it's more than that?"

Lattimore looked at his folded hands for a long moment.

"Mr. Lattimore, we need to know everything you know in order to expedite this case."

Sean glanced at Jennifer again, a little annoyed with her—again—at the impersonal reference she'd just made to a grieving man's ten-year-old son as a "case."

Paul Lattimore finally said, "It's just that, well, when Charlie was going through the worst of it, he had these dreams. He said his mother appeared to him, talked to him, told him that she missed him, but that she was all right. As Emily treated him, they eventually stopped.

"Then about a month ago, I noticed that he started falling into these odd little silences when I'd come into a room, or when we'd be sitting around. He used to do it when he was grappling with those dreams and the depression. A couple of times recently, he closed up entirely after I clearly surprised him on the phone."

"The phone?" Jennifer crossed her arms over her chest and continued to lean against the wall beside the fireplace. "You're telling us that contrary to what you stated before, you *have* been receiving unusual phone calls? Or more importantly, your son has?"

Lattimore's eyes shot to hers, the fear and guilt in them clear.

Sean's gaze settled on Jennifer's too, but the look in his eyes wasn't timid. He waited until Jennifer looked away from Lattimore, connected, and registered his message.

"Just one more thing for now, Paul," he said, letting his eyes linger on Jennifer a moment longer before he looked back at Lattimore. "Did you question Charlie about who it was he was talking to either of those times you surprised him?"

Lattimore was already shaking his head. "No. Emily counseled me to give him room. That advice generally had been working. I didn't want to start contradicting myself now."

"Was anyone else in the house with Charlie who could have intercepted those calls or any others, who might have answered the phone before Charlie took over?"

"Only our housekeeper. She's always with Charlie at the house to watch him whenever I can't be there."

"Okay, then. That's all we need for now. Why don't you go upstairs for a while, rest. We'll keep you informed."

Lattimore pushed himself off the sofa, moving like an old man. His eyes were moist again. "Just tell me this, Sean. Did I screw up? Should I have pressed about those phone calls? Did whoever Charlie was talking to take my boy?"

Sean stood up to walk over to Lattimore. "There's no way we can know that yet, Paul. Don't beat yourself up. You'll only wear yourself down and we need you for this. You with me?"

Lattimore swallowed and tried a weak smile. "Yeah. I am, for anything my son needs. Just get him back to me."

Sean nodded while Lattimore walked away. Then he moved over to the living room table, upon which a state map that nearly covered its circumference had been spread.

"Sheriff," Sean began, perching on the table.

"We're already on it." Mauer nodded to his deputies. "We've put a description of Charlie Lattimore out on the streets, and we're covering this and adjacent neighborhoods to see if anybody saw or heard anything out of the ordinary recently as well as this morning.

"As for the burned woman, her clothes and other pieces of physical evidence from the crime scene have already been sent to the lab for analysis. I'm on my way there to follow up now." He walked over to the chair to reclaim his uniform jacket.

"Thank you." Sean watched the deputies leave the room while Mauer zipped up, then he leaned over the map. The state lay divided into county quadrants, each quadrant bearing a different color shadowing.

"All right, we're going to spread out, start talking to some people." Sean looked at Bob Clemm, the fresh-faced kid who had been transferred from D.C. to the bureau's Southern Indiana office just one year ago.

"Stay close to the hospital. Maurer's men can't be expected to be there all the time, but you can. Talk to the witnesses and staff. See if they've been able to get anything out of the woman yet, or if they're even likely to. Right now, she's our easiest pipeline to all of this, if she lasts."

"Sir," Clemm responded. His clipped tone sounded a little overly enthusiastic inside the darkening room. Mauer looked at the young agent, his eyes amused.

Sean studied Clemm, too, catching the agent's self-conscious flush. He wondered if he'd ever appeared quite that eager or young. He pushed off the table to walk back over to Mauer.

"I appreciate you and your men's cooperation, Sheriff." He held out his hand. Countrywide, bureau alliances with local law enforcement were not always smooth, despite respective supervisory edicts to co-operate. Mauer, though clearly a man of few words, seemed to have made a favorable decision about this situation.

His actions seemed to demonstrate he wasn't going to obstruct, for which Sean was grateful.

"We just want to catch this son-of-a-bitch, whoever he is," Mauer said, accepting Sean's hand in a brief, hard grip. "Lattimore is a good man. Never gets above himself with folks around here, despite who he is. We take care of our own."

Sean nodded. "Thanks," he told Mauer again as the older man left. Back at the table, he turned to the other agent sitting there. "O'Brien, I'd like you to join Clemm at the hospital, assist him with whatever may develop from there. But first, it would help if you could start making calls to Milo's Furniture and Collectibles.

"Talk to the manager, get a read on him, find out how we can get in touch with the dispatcher who gave those delivery men their orders and, allegedly, tracked their progress."

Marty O'Brien, a fifteen-year veteran who, like Sean, had racked up most of his years in the field, was already nodding. "Done."

Finally, Sean turned to Bennett. She sat poised and watchful between Clemm and O'Brien. Her only response to his silent censure from earlier was a faintly raised eyebrow.

"I want to go back to where the truck was found. Bennett, you'll ride with me." He looked at them all. "Anybody got any questions?"

Nobody did.

"Good. Let's take off."

Bennett walked over to the door with the other agents. Sean grabbed his coat from the easy chair he'd vacated earlier and joined her.

"Ready?"

"Sure." She preceded him out into the hallway and through the front door before he could get it for her. He followed, suppressing a humorless smile.

The problem was, he was much better looking than she'd expected. And tougher. Which, annoyingly, only enhanced his physical appeal. Jennifer frowned, irritated with herself for dwelling on such a trivial fact.

Sean Alexander wasn't the first handsome man she'd encountered. He wouldn't be the last. As for the tough demeanor, she'd grown up with military men. Macho deportment, especially in the presence of competing women, wasn't new to her either.

It was just that for some inexplicable reason she'd been thrown by him. First, by his naked reaction to that teddy bear. Next by the way he'd so effortlessly taken charge of Lattimore's questioning and the team, despite the insider bureau talk about his supposed questionable fitness for duty.

She glanced over at him now, noting the way his strongly chiseled features lacked the white winter pallor the other men were starting to take on. His natural coloring carried a faint duskiness that would tan to a striking hue in warmer weather.

In fact, his was an altogether interesting face. Much more so than in the personnel photos and news articles she'd studied on the plane. His deep brown eyes permitted a glimpse into a soul that seemed way too weary for a man of his relative youth.

Cheekbones, whose flatness hinted at an ancestry more Slavic than the distant black Irish clan he'd come from, sat in interesting contrast to the lean, faintly dimpled cheeks, well-formed mouth, and cropped black hair. The entire combination gave him an air of romanticism incongruous with the wiry character his reputation reputed him to be.

His broad hands gripped the steering wheel now with competence and confidence. Involuntarily, Jennifer had a flashing image of them on the delicate skin of a woman's spine as they contoured their way down to more intimate contact.

Jesus. She did *not* need to be thinking about Sean Alexander this way.

"Something wrong?" Sean asked, wondering at the impatience in her breathy exhalation.

"Not at all," Jennifer responded coolly.

"Good, because I want to know something."

"What's that?"

"Are we going to have a problem?"

"What?"

"I said, are we going to have a problem? I thought I sensed a bit of one-upsmanship back there at the house."

"You're mistaken—"

"When you started giving Lattimore a hard time."

"Listen, just because I pushed a little when you had already decided to go easy on a man who clearly needed to be prodded—"

"Whoa. Where's this coming from?"

Jennifer took a breath, resettling herself. "I don't know what you're talking about."

And all at once, another piece about Jennifer Bennett clicked into place. She was rumored to be Anthony Collins's pet, yes. But her name also had passed the lips of some of the older agents who knew her as one of Sean's most vocal internal critics among the new crop of agents.

Brash, beautiful, brilliant. And ambitious. A star in the making, just like he'd been *before*. "It's about the bear, about what seeing it may have done to me, isn't it?"

Jennifer turned to face him. "Yes. But my reaction probably isn't what you're thinking."

"Tell me what I'm thinking." In spite of his annoyance, Sean liked the way she didn't flinch.

Jennifer shrugged, looking out her window. "You think I'm one of those agents who criticized you in the aftermath, and maybe to an extent that's true. You think I did it because of what happened. That's not true."

"Go on."

"You played it as well as anyone could have, right up to that awful end. Not even the professionals on the hostage negotiation team had gotten as far as you had with Albert Brady. They hadn't won his trust the way you clearly had.

"When you actually got him away from his gang and outside that schoolroom for a face-to-face negotiation, well, it was impressive to say the least." And it still was in retrospect, Jennifer thought, remembering how she and just about every other agent in the bureau had been riveted, awed—and in her case, maybe a little envious—by the televised spectacle.

"But he blew the school anyway," Sean pointed out. "So what did all my 'success' up to then really mean?"

"It meant that until that happened, you were able to establish a dialogue with the terrorists a team of seasoned hostage negotiators couldn't. It meant that for a few hours right before the end, you had those terrorists reconsidering, which meant those children honestly had a chance.

"It means the way you took control of the negotiation and handled yourself demonstrated you truly were as good as the stories I'd heard about you from the day I hit basic training. The impossible image I and every other cadet were silently encouraged to live up to wasn't just talk, but something very potent and real."

"Ah. And so when you and your fellow cadets saw the legend spectacularly fail despite all that, it dashed your starry dreams, is that it?"

"No, it's not, I'm not disillusioned that easily. No one could have guessed Brady was going to detonate that bomb because there was absolutely no reason in the world why he should have. But you couldn't see that, you of all people. So you walked away from the job."

Sean made a disgusted sound. "You think it's that easy? Sean Alexander failed in front of a nation and his ego couldn't handle it?"

"You had to be dragged onto this case, didn't you?" And she knew she'd revealed too much by the quick way he looked at her, by the absolute cynicism in his smile.

"So, it's true what they say about you and Collins. Tell me, Special Agent Bennett, were you handpicked? Did you agree to come on board, not because the life of an innocent ten-year-old is at stake, but rather because maybe this is your big chance?"

Stung because she couldn't fully deny it, Jennifer said, "Go to hell."

"Lady, I've already been there. And if your wide eyes can't let you imagine what I'm really talking about, we *will* have a problem." He came to a narrow, tree-flanked lane and turned. A few yards ahead, they saw the blackened shell of the delivery truck and a smattering of state police cars surrounding it. Sean parked along the side of the road, then cut the engine.

With his hands still on the steering wheel, he pinned her with hard eyes. "Tell me now."

Jennifer, just as angry, just as cool, stated, "I've already answered that question. But for the record, since you insist, you don't get in my way and I'll stay out of yours." She got out of the car.

Chapter Four

The site report was both frustrating and encouraging. No third body had been found. However, along the side of the road bullet casings had been recovered.

Clearly, a pistol had to have been fired in order to have ejected them. Just as clearly, chances were they weren't the leavings of some game hunter whose shooting had gone amuck along the side of a commercial road.

Additionally, blood traces had been found along the road not far from the casings. They, too, were being analyzed. Neither Sean nor Jennifer doubted the blood was human.

Jennifer knew these revelations, though inconclusive, should have been cause for some excitement. Instead, her thoughts ran on a slightly different track as she and Sean drove back to Paul Lattimore's retreat where he'd invited them to spend the night.

In all the time they'd been at the truck site, Sean

hadn't said a word to her beyond what he had to. His icy control was starting to unnerve her, but she didn't dare let him know.

She sensed how easily another misstep could cost her more footing. If you called footing what she'd gained.

She didn't think so. In fact, their earlier exchange had left her feeling vaguely depressed, and she didn't like feeling that way when her head told her she'd been right to speak her mind plainly.

Still . . .

The car phone beeped. Sean palmed it and pressed it on.

"Yeah," his voice still sounded clipped to Jennifer. He glanced at her, asking the caller, "Will I like it?"

Jennifer waited anxiously for more. Sean didn't give it, though he held onto the phone. Finally, he said, "We're headed back to Lattimore's if you get more before morning. Yeah." Still one-handed, he severed the connection. "That was Mauer," was all he said, then he resettled the phone beneath the dash.

"What did he have?" Jennifer sighed inwardly, not wanting to have to pull the details.

"The gun used was a thirty-eight-caliber semi-automatic pistol. The bullet type matches the one recovered from Jane Doe at the hospital. The blood on the pavement was indeed human, although its type, O negative, does not match that of Jane Doe in the

76

hospital, or of Charlie Lattimore, whose type is B. It appears we're looking for a third party who, in all likelihood, wasn't one of the real store delivery men, although the blood data will be cross-checked against their types to either support or discourage that presumption."

"If one of the men wasn't one of the original delivery men—"

"Precisely. Odds become neither of them were, which means maybe we should be looking for two missing bodies instead of one. A local team will be out here combing the area with that in mind, first thing in the morning.

Jennifer nodded. "That's good." She was watching his set face. "But that's not all, is it?"

"Another report came in. Charlie Lattimore's blood wasn't the blood on that teddy bear. The sample on the bear tested positive as animal blood. Feline, to be exact."

Jennifer sighed, feeling relieved. "Thank God for that." When Sean lapsed back into silence, she looked at him. He watched the road. His grip on the steering wheel didn't relax.

"Listen," she began.

Sean glanced at her, then back at the road.

"I didn't mean to offend you with what I said. It's just that you put me on the spot. I got defensive."

"I hope that's a flaw you're working on."

It was a flaw. Her temper always had been. In light of that, she couldn't honestly say much to defend herself against his calm observation. The atmosphere in the car was as chilly as the night air outside.

Sean finally said, "Necessity is going to keep us pretty close on this. If we spend all our time sniping at each other, this assignment's going to get impossible in a hurry."

"I agree," Jennifer said readily. She was grateful he'd provided the opening she hadn't been able to.

"So I propose this. I'll extend the olive branch if you'll accept it."

She already took it as a promising sign that he, too, hated the unease between them enough to make the offer. "Fair enough," she told him.

"All right."

The rest of the drive, if not companionable, was at least palpably less tense.

Once inside Lattimore's house, they both declined a formal meal. Instead they ate sandwiches the housekeeper fixed for them in the kitchen. After that, they said their good nights and Jennifer climbed the stairs, heading for the room she'd been given for the night.

Sean started to follow to his own, then changed his mind. Impulsively, he headed back to the now empty living room.

*   *   *

At the wet bar, he found a decanter of Scotch and a glass. He poured himself a finger. Somebody had ignited the logs in the fireplace. With all of the lights out inside the room, the fire's glow enhanced the room's hushed, contemplative atmosphere. Sean's mood reflected the surroundings perfectly.

He settled himself in one of the easy chairs flanking the hearth and raised his whiskey to his mouth. The liquid bit as it slid down his throat, and he welcomed the calming sensation as companion to his thoughts.

Feline. Not Charlie Lattimore's. Which meant only one thing he knew neither he—nor this investigation—could deny.

The bear, combined with the Irish reference in the ransom note, had been meant for him. And whoever left them had Charlie Lattimore. Somehow, the sadistic message was linked to him.

Charlie Lattimore contemplated his prison. About three hours ago the nature of it had changed from the car to this single room. Now he lay in the dark on his back on a hard little bed.

As he'd promised, the man had bought them both McDonald's drive-thru food, but not before he'd made Charlie climb inside the trunk of the car. Once they had their food, the man had driven a short distance before letting Charlie up front again.

After that, they'd found a gas station at the side of the road. Its near emptiness had spared Charlie a return to the musty trunk. But he'd still had to scrunch down on the floor under the dashboard while the man pumped the gas, then went inside to pay for it at the tiny white brick convenience island Charlie had seen before he'd knelt out of sight.

They'd driven along a series of backroads, all headed north, all mostly deserted except for a couple of speeding cars with older kids behind the wheel. The man had finally pulled off the road and onto the tiny overgrown asphalt parking lot of a deserted park. A peeling picnic bench was nestled in amidst some trees and patchy grass.

They'd eaten their food there without a single word between them, except for when the man had asked, "You want some of this?" then, "Here's some ketchup to go with those."

After they'd finished eating, they'd tossed their trash into a nearby rusty bin and had gotten back on the road. They'd stayed there until the skyscrapers of downtown Indianapolis appeared in the distance.

The man had made Charlie climb inside the trunk again. Except this time, he'd made him stay there for what seemed like hours.

When Charlie had been let out and able to see his watch, he'd seen he'd been confined for only a little under one hour. But it was as fully dark by then outside the trunk as it had been inside that tiny space. And the deserted state roads were gone.

The man had brought him to a house.

It was small and single-story, red brick with white shutters. The lawn was deep in the front and had been neatly mowed. The fallen leaves from the two oak trees there had been raked. Charlie's main focus of interest, however, didn't promise much.

The house was surrounded by acres of land with no other houses within close sight. A rutted unpaved road ran in front of the house. On the other side of the road lay acres of field, enclosed by a sagging wire mesh fence.

From drives with his father, Charlie had learned this kind of land was what you saw when there were mostly cows and horses. Maybe pigs. Maybe even some goats.

But few people. And now the man was taking him inside the back door, through the kitchen, down a set of narrow steps, and into a basement. By the light the man switched on at the top of the stairs, Charlie saw that the basement had been converted into a bedroom.

His room for the next few days, the man told him. Then he'd pointed out the narrow bed with a cloth-covered table and lamp beside it, a bookshelf that had some kids' books Charlie thought were more for babies than boys his age, and a ladder-backed wooden chair beside the table.

There also was a corner of the room that had been sectioned off from the rest by a plywood wall. Behind it was a toilet and sink that obviously had been newly installed.

Charlie didn't know what he was supposed to say, so he watched the man's face as all of this was explained to him. The man looked expectant. Charlie tried a smile. The man smiled back. Charlie knew to keep playing along.

Finally, the man had gestured all around them with widespread arms and asked Charlie if he liked it. Charlie, still smiling, had said yes. He'd nodded when the man had asked him if the covers on the bed were going to be warm enough for him. Then Charlie asked if he could have a drink of water. He knew his question had pleased the man when he actually chuckled and walked over to the sectioned off little bathroom.

Charlie heard him run some water from there, then he brought back a filled plastic cup. Charlie drained it, careful to say a polite thank-you. That's when the man had simply said, "See you in the morning." Then he'd gone away. Back up the stairs, through the door, and Charlie had heard him turn the key in the shiny gold lock he'd noticed on the other side of the door.

Charlie had lain on his temporary bed then—where the covers *weren't* warm enough—thinking about what else he had noticed outside. It was something the man hadn't pointed out.

At the bottom of the side of the house was a small rectangular window. Charlie knew it had to be at the top of one of the basement walls. Inside this converted room, however, he'd seen no sign of that window.

He *had* noticed that the four walls of the room absorbed sound very well.

The way the man's voice carried to nowhere was almost like listening to him speak inside a sealed room.

Which maybe this was. It would only make sense that the man would soundproof the room so that his prisoner wouldn't be heard from the outside. That meant some kind of insulation was probably behind the walls.

Which meant that window he couldn't find also had to be somewhere under that insulation.

Charlie finally let his eyes drift closed. His body was tired from the effects of whatever that woman had injected him with.

The window. Tomorrow, finding it was going to become his project. He was going to find a way to see the light of day one way or another.

Nine-thirty p.m.

Sean roused, immediately sensing he wasn't alone. He sat up a little straighter in the soft chair he'd fallen asleep in. The fire, though low, still burned. On the adjacent sofa was another person, quietly watching him.

"Paul, it's late. What are you doing here?" Sean got up to stretch a little, then walked back over to the bar. He refilled his glass with water and carried it back to his chair.

"It's been a long time, Sean. Years too long. I thought we needed to talk, to get some things out in the open."

Sean drank his water, watching Paul's eyes glow in the fire's light. He finally turned his gaze back to the softly crackling fire.

Lattimore said, "I tried to say I'm sorry years ago and you wouldn't listen. I'm asking you again. Will you now? Listen?"

"Did Cheryl after you hit her? The second time? Or the third?"

Paul Lattimore didn't respond for a long time. He fell to watching the flames, too, before finally answering. "She did, eventually. I was a complete fool, Sean. No one despised my behavior more than I did. The miracle was, she actually came to understand that and to believe it. And to finally love me again."

"She always did, Paul. She and I were through long before you two ever began. There was nothing stronger than friendship between us by the time you two met."

"I know that now." Lattimore sighed. "A man's jealousy can be a terrible thing. The very objects he wants to protect and love can end up being the very things he destroys."

"Only if he tries to possess them. And Cheryl was never a possession. Either mine or yours."

"But in those first years after Charlie was born, she said things that made me believe she wanted to be yours. You have to know that, don't you, Sean?"

Sean did know it. But the recognition still filled him with sadness rather than the guilt it could have had he reciprocated Cheryl Lattimore's feelings.

He lapsed into silent contemplation. He recalled the time he, Paul, and Cheryl had met. He recalled the time even before that.

Sean, his parents, and his older brother, Robert, had all come to Boston when Sean was ten, after years of living in England. In England, his parents had raised their boys in modest comfort as first-generation émigrés from Northern Ireland.

Outside a few Irish traditions comfortably observed inside his home, Sean's upbringing was thoroughly working-class English. And that design was aided by the fact—to his parents' relief—that his immediate relatives preferred to stay in the old country.

His homelife had been carefully arranged by his parents to be what they envisioned would become a safe existence, free from the threat of political street violence they had fled. And within that life, Sean grew up surviving the ordinary scrapes, pranks, and jams bright, daring little boys got into.

Unfortunately, it was Robert who possessed a streak wild enough to lure him to straddle the politically unsettled line between England and their embattled homeland.

It was after sixteen-year-old Robert nearly got himself killed in a raid on a church, a raid perpetrated by buddies in the IRA he'd halfheartedly joined, that their parents decided to uproot once again for the sake of protecting their boys.

Robert's brush with violent death left more than just a scare with the family. It left an impression on Sean that would last him a lifetime. While he continued to enjoy a good scrap with the American boys who became his new friends, his gut-deep aversion to stark violence, to random and senseless cruelty, had been born.

By the time Sean finished high school, Robert had chosen his path in life, surprisingly nothing more complex than the kind of working-class life their parents lived. He had talented hands, so construction absorbed his energies until he was able to open up a profitable little firm of his own in Boston.

Sean, however, went to college, still seeking a direction for his own life. Unfocused though he was, he was fairly certain whatever he chose would center around the law. Which was why the first profession he attempted to formally explore *was* the law.

Two years into law school he realized the elusive something he wanted from his studies was incompatible with the rigid fields of either litigation or legal research that a degree promised. So he dropped out, leaving his impressive grades and regretful professors behind. He decided to give the grittier prospect of city policing a try.

He lasted two more years before the same dissatisfaction, this time with the repetitive paperwork and procedural limitations of the job, kicked in.

That's when he considered the Federal Bureau of Investigation. It sounded like policing, with the added lure of edginess and investigatory latitude the streets hadn't offered him.

Almost from the beginning, the bureau had been the right fit. Sean had always had a talent for thinking out of the box, as his instructors liked to say. That talent was what had made him an exceptional law student. It also was what, in short order, made him an exceptionally intuitive agent.

Within a year after he'd earned his federal shield,

he'd been posted in Washington. It was in a Georgetown college pub that he'd met Cheryl Robinson, a political science major at the university.

The speed and intensity of their attraction had surprised them both. It also had kept them enthralled with each other for weeks afterward. But like a flame that flares too brightly to endure, so did their affair.

Fundamentally one of passion, it burned for a short while before it simply flickered and winked out. Sean wasn't heartbroken. Neither was Cheryl. They'd both seen the end coming long before it had arrived.

Also, by that time Sean had noticed Cheryl's eyes wandering to a new friend of his, Paul Lattimore, a junior congressman a mutual friend had introduced him to at a party.

Seeing that her attention was reciprocated, and being genuinely fond of both friends, Sean had simply made the formal introduction each clearly desired.

In short order, the course of love between Paul and Cheryl and the marriage that resulted seemed to run, as the poets were wont to say, steady and true.

In the seven years that followed, Sean built his career and his reputation through several field office postings across the country. He was living in Indianapolis and into his second year as special-agent-in-charge of the field office there when he received the letter from Cheryl.

She and Paul had moved to Indiana. Their reasons were twofold. First, they'd decided to develop some property Cheryl's recently deceased father had left to her as an inheritance. Second, they'd decided to downscale the fast-paced Capitol Hill lives they'd been living during the years of Paul's service in the United States Senate.

And, Cheryl candidly revealed, their motivation behind the downscale had more to do with her having recently been diagnosed with breast cancer than their actually wanting to move.

Her chances for survival, she wrote, were judged only even at best.

Shaken, Sean had gone immediately to their new home to offer his support for anything they needed. The last thing he had expected was Cheryl's taking him up on his promise in an unexpected way.

He'd been spending an afternoon with them at their sprawling house in a very upscale suburb of the city. It had been a comfortably casual time for reacquaintance and renewal. The three of them had spent the day lazing around the pool.

It was early evening when Sean went back inside to the spare guest room he'd used earlier to change out of his street clothes. He'd not heard Cheryl quietly enter behind him.

Not questioning her presence at first, Sean had rushed to her, fearing that she was feeling ill, maybe even in pain. Only when she'd moved firmly inside his embrace and suddenly pressed her lips to his did he realize how he had let his vulnerability to a sensitive situation set him up as a target for trouble.

He'd pushed her away gently, hating the hurt in her eyes, the pleading in her voice.

"He doesn't love me anymore, Sean," she'd protested. "He loves his job. He hates like hell that I forced him to leave it."

"Cheryl, I'm sure you're wrong—" But she had started crying. She didn't make a sound, just watched him hopelessly while the tears ran down her face.

Unable to hold her away while she was gripped by this emotional pain, Sean was the one who drew her close this time, offering comfort.

"He doesn't—he doesn't even touch me anymore, Sean," she whispered. "He can't bear it, the thought of my illness, this disease."

Sean didn't know what to say. He closed his eyes and absorbed her tears against his shirt as she rested her head on his chest.

Of course that's when Paul walked in, misconstruing everything. He called his wife names he'd regret until his dying day. He called his friend worse, then ordered him to leave their house.

Sean did, overlooking Cheryl's tearful protests for him to stay. He realized, even if Cheryl didn't, that no explanation to Paul had a chance of succeeding until all their heads were cooler and their emotions weren't running so high.

But even after two days had passed, Paul still had rejected Sean's attempt to explain his wife's distress. More surprising to Sean, Cheryl ceased communicating with him, too. He eventually decided whatever solution to their problem evolved, it was ultimately going to have to be something worked out between the two of them.

But two months later, Cheryl's second letter had arrived. The restlessness of it was similar to her first. And she'd inserted an additional detail. Paul had hit her.

It seemed after all this time, Paul still hadn't let go of his suspicions about them. It wasn't so much that he brooded upon what he hadn't caught them doing that day at the house. Rather, it was Paul's certainty of what he felt they had wanted to do then, and still did now.

Agitated, Sean had made the trip he knew Cheryl wanted him to make to the Lattimore house. He'd found Paul alone, in the flower garden behind the house. He'd confronted him about the abusiveness Cheryl alleged. Paul's only reaction had been anger over the fact that Cheryl had exposed their marital problems to "an outsider," which is what he now called Sean.

"Stay out of our lives, leave my wife alone!" Paul

had shouted. She was his business, and he'd treat her any way he saw fit. That wild remark had incensed Sean like none of Paul's earlier foolishness had. The two men had nearly come to blows when Cheryl came hurrying into the garden to investigate the commotion.

But instead of being indignant against her husband, she had rushed to his side, as she had done, Sean recalled, once before. She had taken his arm and, too, asked Sean to leave.

Frustrated, Sean had done so, conscious all the while of the regret in Cheryl's eyes.

That was the last time he had ever heard from Cheryl Lattimore. That was also the last time he had ever seen her alive. After her funeral, he hadn't seen Paul again.

Until now.

Sean sipped his water, waiting for Paul to say something.

"What can I say? I was out of my mind, Sean. I loved her so much. The fact that she turned to you and not me about our problems just tore me apart. I shouldn't have taken my frustrations out on her. I knew it then just as I know it now."

Sean kept listening.

"The miracle is, in the end she forgave me. I came down here tonight to ask you if you could do the same. Not just for Charlie's sake, but for ours—yours and mine—as one-time friends."

Sean studied Paul Lattimore's eyes. He saw a suffering and tiredness of spirit in them he knew too well. And all at once, beyond the old anger and wounded pain, he just felt tired.

He set his glass down on the hearthstone at his feet and leaned forward. And held out his hand.

Paul Lattimore shut his eyes tightly and gripped that hand with his own.

"It has been too long," Sean finally said. Then after letting a few more moments pass, he added, "My friend."

Jennifer backed away from the doorway. The book she'd come hunting as a remedy to help her sleep was forgotten. Instead, unseen, she gathered her robe more securely around her and pondered the private moment she had just witnessed.

She hadn't heard all that had preceded it, but she'd heard enough to be thrown off balance again. Suddenly in the blink of an eye, the Lattimores—Charlie, his father, even his dead wife—had taken on a reality and humanity Jennifer hadn't wanted them to.

She wasn't proud to admit it, but a part of her always needed to stay cold to situations that demanded the best work from her. That distance was a professional necessity as well as a characteristic of her personal makeup. She'd accepted it, even conditioned herself to respect it.

Now, she had the uncomfortable feeling her customary detachment was going to be tested. And her certainty had everything to do with the unexpectedness of Sean Alexander.

He appeared to be far from the emotional burnout she and others had speculated he was.

She was beginning to suspect the truth was Sean Alexander felt too much. He had a seeming capacity for the sort of emotional intensity that drew her even while it frightened her.

Jennifer slowly retraced her path through the hallway and back up the stairs to her room.

Chapter Five

Day Two
Seven a.m.

The sound of the key turning in the lock woke Charlie.

He kept his eyes shut while the basement door opened. He didn't know what the man had in store, but maybe if the man thought he was still asleep he'd turn around and leave again.

Charlie heard him walk down the steps and across the basement floor. He kept breathing evenly while the man came over to the side of the bed and stood there, Charlie imagined, just looking down at him. Then the man coughed.

Charlie didn't move.

"Are you awake?" the man asked, suddenly.

Charlie jumped when the man shook him. Sighing, he rolled onto his back and opened his eyes.

"Here, I brought you some breakfast." The man set a tray on the table beside the bed. Then he bent a little, feeling for the switch along the bottom of the lamp, which he turned on.

Charlie blinked at the sudden light. He scooted up against the brick wall behind the bed, which served as his headboard. He looked at the man warily, still not saying anything.

The man looked back at him, an unreadable expression on his face.

Charlie glanced at the tray. A bowl of oatmeal, a slice of toast, buttered, a small glass of orange juice. And a pitcher of ice water. There was a spoon, a plastic cup, and a napkin, too.

"Go ahead, you have to be hungry. You haven't eaten since yesterday afternoon." The man looked as if he were going to sit along the side of the bed before he changed his mind. Instead, he leaned against the wall and crossed his arms.

Only then did Charlie notice that he was dressed for work. A lightweight brown suit, beige shirt, brown striped tie, brown loafers. His light hair was neatly combed back from his forehead and brows, and even looked like it had some kind of gel in it. His pale eyes didn't blink.

He should have looked classy. Instead, Charlie could only think of a snake again. And the longer

Charlie stared at him, the more his expression stilled like a reptile about to strike.

"I said, eat it, kid. It's all you'll get until I get home this afternoon."

Startled, Charlie pushed the light blanket that covered him off his legs and brought his feet to the side of the bed. Still watching the man, he reached over to the tray and picked up the toast, looked at it, then took a tiny bite.

Despite his resistance, his mouth watered at the taste of the warm bread and he began to chew. He took another bite, then another, until the toast was gone.

The man smiled. "Good." He still didn't move away from the wall, still didn't uncross his arms. Only his mouth moved, and his eyes narrowed a little. "Now the oatmeal."

Again, Charlie's hunger battled his will. He didn't want to give the man the satisfaction of eating, but his stomach growled. Slowly, he picked up the spoon, then the bowl. Then he scooped up a spoonful of the cereal, which was thicker than he'd ever had it, and put it in his mouth. Surprisingly, it was good. Sweet, still warm, and he could taste the butter in it.

He took another spoonful, then another, eating quickly now, the goodness of the food making him rush through it. When he was down to the last bit of it, he started to put the bowl down when the man said, "All of it."

Charlie looked up at him. The man was still smiling, but his eyes were intent. At that moment, Charlie felt a faint wave of dizziness that passed almost as soon as it came upon him. He got a sinking feeling in his stomach.

"You put something in it, didn't you?" he accused.

The man's smile transformed into an expression of regret. "I didn't want you getting restless while I was gone. Or lonely. This way, you'll sleep."

"I don't *want* to sleep." He was thinking about the window, about his plans to find the window!

The man came away from the wall and this time didn't hesitate to sit on the side of the bed. Charlie scooted away, watching him, afraid he was going to hurt him.

The man read the fear in Charlie's eyes. His smile slipped. He held out a hand, inviting Charlie to move back over. Then he seemed to think better of it, and let his hand drop to the blanket. "Remember what I told you yesterday? That I didn't want to harm you?"

Charlie fought a childish urge to cry. He nodded uneasily instead.

"I didn't lie to you, Charlie. I've never lied to you and I never will. I'll treat you right as long as you don't *make* me hurt you. Do you understand?"

Charlie wasn't entirely sure, so he nodded again.

The man watched him, saying nothing as a hard glint came into his eye. Suddenly, he reached across the bed and grabbed Charlie roughly by the shoulders. Shaking him, he said sharply, "*What* do you understand?"

"That I have to be a good boy!" Charlie gasped. "That I have to not make you mad." *Because you're crazy*, he added to himself.

As suddenly as he'd grown angry, the man turned calm again. His bruising grip on Charlie's arms loosened. He took one of his hands away to brush at the bangs that had fallen over Charlie's eyes. "How could I be mad at my boy? You're so good, aren't you? Just perfect."

Charlie watched him, swallowing, feeling very small in the loose yet viselike grip. Then, the man released him and stood up.

Charlie scooted back against the wall. Another wave of dizziness hit him. This time when it receded he felt drowsy. His head started to droop as he heard the man say, "I have to go to work now. If you wake up you won't be bored. You've got those books I put on the shelf for you over there. They're your favorites."

Charlie fought to keep his eyes open. Favorites? What was he talking about? He tried to ask but somehow thought it easier to let his body slide back down onto the mattress. It was easier just to pull the cover back up and close his eyes.

The last thing he heard before the scrape of the key in the lock was soft laughter.

She couldn't see. She could hear herself breathing, could hear a steady beeping coming from somewhere in the distance. But she couldn't open her eyes. She panicked and tried to say something, unaware that the only sound she made was a tiny moan.

"What was that? Honey, are you awake?" The nurse moved closer to the burn victim's bedside. Sterile gauze bandages were still packed heavily against her face, neck, and torso where she'd received the worst of her burn injuries. She'd not regained consciousness since she'd been brought in. It appeared that situation was about to change.

Judy heard the excited young voice, but it was as if she were hearing it from a distance, as if the same padding that pressed against her face and neck was stuffed inside her ears, muting the sounds around her. She tried to speak again.

The young nurse's aid listened to the victim's faint moans, wondering if she should get a doctor. "Wait right here, honey. I'll call someone for you."

Judy tried to tell her not to go, not to leave her alone. *Alone.* She was alone.

From the recesses of her memory, she heard the

gunshot. Felt the searing pain that downed her where she stood. Felt the horror of Roy grabbing her legs to pull her backward, to finish the job his bullet had started.

Tears welled in her eyes before they overflowed. But she couldn't feel them on her face, couldn't feel their warm moisture on her cheeks.

Then another kind of fear hit her. Why couldn't she feel her face? Why couldn't she speak, or move, or open her eyes to see? Or even hear properly? Maybe she was dreaming. Maybe she was already dead. Like Hal. *Hal . . . !*

"What's that she's saying?" Bob Clemm leaned further over the protective railing, conscious of the sterile gown and mask and cap he wore, trying to catch the faint sound coming from Jane Doe's lips.

"Sounds like 'how,' " the doctor answered. "Probably she's asking how she got this way. No wonder. Anybody hurt like that who suddenly regained even this partial consciousness would want to know what the hell was going on."

Bob Clemm listened to the doctor's explanation while he continued to watch the woman. Jane Doe's eyes stayed closed. Finally, her lips stilled, too.

"She's out again," the doctor said, and sighed. "Probably best. Her pain would be pretty bad if she were awake to feel it."

Bob Clemm took a step back. "How's her condition this morning, Doc?"

The doctor shrugged, looking down at the woman. "The burns are serious. But even aside from those, that gunshot wound did a lot of damage when it exited. We've had to do a partial removal of her lower left lung. Combined with the shock and other trauma she's sustained, she's not good."

"Is she going to make it?"

"The next twenty-four hours or so should tell us."

Clemm looked at his watch. He needed to check in with O'Brien, to coordinate their plan for the day, which probably meant interviews in Indianapolis. He started toward the door, lowering his mask and loosening the ties to his gown as he walked.

"If there's any other change in her condition, if she says anything else or seems to be waking up, call me. My number's at the nurse's station. That means you and your nurses all should use it no matter how late or early that may be."

The doctor was nodding. "You've got it," she said to his back.

After Clemm was gone, she turned back to the burned woman. If she woke up?

Though it was sacrilegious to her professional oath, the doctor couldn't help thinking, with those kinds of injuries, why would she want to wake up?

* * *

"When are you leaving for Indianapolis, Paul?" Sean slipped his sunglasses on and walked to the front door where Jennifer stood.

Lattimore glanced at his watch. "In about an hour or so. I just have a few more of Charlie's things to pack."

Sean and Jennifer watched him.

"Some books that are his favorites, some video games, his other jacket, things like that. He'll need them when he comes home."

Jennifer turned to Sean, who met her look briefly before saying to Lattimore, "Okay. You can reach either one of us through the field office there, day or night. Of course, we'll stay in touch with anything that breaks."

"I'm counting on it."

Sean nodded. "Don't let Emily Marsh know we're coming. We need her responses to be spontaneous, her answers unrehearsed."

"Of course. Whatever's best. Just—"

"Yes?" Jennifer prompted.

"Emily's special. Don't give her a hard time. If it weren't for her after Cheryl died, I don't know what I would have done with Charlie."

"We'll do our best," Sean said.

Inside the car, Jennifer waited until Sean started the engine. "You think that was ordinary concern for his son's therapist or something else?"

"Like?"

"Extraordinary concern for the woman, not the shrink."

Sean started down the drive. "The reason for your speculation is?"

Jennifer shrugged. "What would Paul Lattimore have to gain by his son's disappearance?"

"What you're really wondering is," Sean glanced at her, "if Paul Lattimore stands to benefit financially from his son's death."

Jennifer looked over at him. His expression was unreadable. "Yeah. That's what I'm saying."

"A possibility, of course." Sean's voice was cool. "And in addition to everything else, it deserves to be checked out. But I'll tell you now, my gut tells me that line of thinking leads down a false path."

"Because he's your friend?"

"Because Paul Lattimore isn't a killer. He's brash, impulsive, headstrong, passionate. The career and reputation he values so highly evolved from his being all of those things. But he's also devoted to his son."

Jennifer let that thought settle. "What, precisely, did you mean by everything else?" She thought about it, then answered herself. "The bear."

"The bear."

"Let's talk about it."

"Let's do it over food."

Jennifer didn't object. She sat quietly with her thoughts while Sean rode with his.

On the town's main drag, Jennifer spotted a family restaurant whose reputation 'relied upon being open all night. Inside, after they were seated and their orders were brought to them, Jennifer started picking at her food. Halfway through, as Sean just continued to eat, Jennifer broke the silence. "So, what do you think, Sean Alexander? Who are your enemies?"

Where the hell *was* it? Not in the living room, not in any of the table drawers, under the sofa cushions, stuffed in any of the magazines scattered around the floor. He'd checked the back bedroom area, which meant checking the only piece of furniture in there, the bed. It wasn't under her mattress.

Judy had always written things down since they were kids. She'd always kept notes in journals, letters, diaries, spiral notebook entries. That's why he knew she had to have left *something* in 'here now, something spelling out exactly where they were taking the kid. He hadn't been in on that part. He was just supposed to be waiting at this point, waiting for his money.

There had to be something for him to get his hands on that detailed where that bastard Roy had the boy.

Because Roy had killed Hal. And according to the

news reports this morning he had tried to kill Judy, who they were calling Jane Doe.

Well, *he* was going to kill Roy. When he found him. For Hal. For Judy. For their money.

He stood in the living room, trying to figure it out. He hadn't expected a double cross. Or for Hal and Judy to pay for it.

Ten million dollars was a lot of money and he wasn't about to be gypped out of at least his cut. Or his revenge. Roy, for all his mild-mannered looks, wanted to play rough? Well, he didn't know what rough could be. But he'd find out, as soon as *he* found out where Roy and the kid were holed up.

There'll be hell to pay, Roy, he thought. And that hell's gonna be me.

Marty O'Brien got out of his car and made his way across the dew-damp slope of grass leading down to where Sheriff Mauer, state police, and crime lab technicians were standing around a police van. O'Brien took in the intense expressions on their faces. "Sheriff," he greeted Mauer when he reached the group.

Mauer turned, recognizing him from their meeting at Lattimore's estate. He held out a hand.

"Here awfully early aren't you?" O'Brien said, shaking it.

Mauer raised his brows over eyes that looked a

little grim. "As long as that boy is missing, it isn't early."

O'Brien silently agreed, liking Mauer's answer. "So, what do we have?"

"A plan to spread out and cover a few miles in each direction here. See what turns up. We have a fair idea it could be a body or bodies, given the blood and ballistics evidence." He took in O'Brien's neatly tailored dark blue suit, pristine white shirt, burgundy tie. "You planning on joining in here this morning?"

"No, I'm on my way to Indianapolis, to the store that made Lattimore's delivery. Just thought I'd stop by first to see if any information freebies had turned up that might help me."

"Hopefully later, but not yet. You know I'll call you if we find something."

O'Brien looked at him, wondering if he was being snide by the if-you-need-to-know qualification. Mauer looked right back at him, his eyes clear. Satisfied, O'Brien stepped back, glancing beyond Mauer to the uniformed men and women who had begun to fan out. "You got any kids, Sheriff?"

Mauer looked his officers over too. His eyes narrowed a little. "Yes. Two teenage girls and a boy who's a little older. I don't know what I'd do if I turned around one day and they were gone." He paused, "Especially if I'd already lost my wife."

"Like Lattimore."

"Exactly like. He loved that woman. Mind you, they had their problems same as everybody else. But you couldn't doubt the feeling was there, especially toward the end." Mauer looked back at O'Brien. "She was too young. It was sad."

"I understand little Charlie had some problems dealing with her death, too. Did Lattimore ever have any special problems with Charlie's wandering alone around the estate?"

"Problems?"

"He and his father are high-profile personalities. I know Lattimore's careful about his security around the grounds. Still, security obviously can be breached. Any other incidents, especially recent, of that sort of thing happening?"

Mauer was already shaking his head. "No. The isolation out here is one of the reasons the Lattimores chose to develop this land. Neither ever reported any troubles with prowlers or gawkers. In fact, most people around here probably don't even know exactly where their place is."

"You're saying most people who live in the vicinity don't know about their famous neighbors? Or just that they aren't curious enough to intrude?"

"The Lattimore property is pretty isolated, and they've always valued maintaining their privacy. Sure, most people know they have a house in the county, but aside from that their nearest neighbors around here in any direction are at least a mile away.

"A couple of cabins within that mile are inhabited. But they're clean. We searched them and questioned their owners. Other than that, you get occasional squatters around here, transients who come and go through the shelters they throw up in the woods."

"Their regular neighbors, though. They didn't see or hear anything unusual leading up to or following the truck fire?"

"That's what they say."

"Do you find that plausible?"

"Considering who these people are, yeah. One guy's a wood-carver, an artsy type who frequently goes off alone to fish and commune in the woods even further south of here. That's where he was yesterday morning when that truck started burning. He says he didn't get back until sometime between one and two in the afternoon."

"And his story checks out?"

"It does. The owner of the pay fishing lake he says he was at vouches for him during the hours of the morning he says he was there. The gas attendant of the station where he says he stopped to fill up his tank on the way home does the same for the time he says he made the stop."

"And the other neighbor?"

"A lawyer. She's out of town at a convention, a

story that checks, too. The warrant we got to search her cabin didn't turn up anything."

O'Brien nodded. With the regulars who lived here and the ones who were traipsing through, somebody surely had to have seen something out of the ordinary. Even if they didn't realize it. He didn't want to step on local toes, but he'd run it by Sean later, see if he agreed these neighbors were worth questioning again.

"Well, then, I'll leave you to it," O'Brien said.

Mauer raised an acknowledging hand.

O'Brien made his way back down the slope to the side of the road and his parked car.

"Lots of people lost someone," Sean answered, forking off a bite of his pancakes. "When you consider the spectrum of who that could mean, you have relatives of the living, relatives of the dead, critics of the entire rescue operation, an assortment of others who could be motivated by who knows what. Lots of people."

"But has anyone who might fit into any of those categories surfaced to make themselves known in the year since it happened? Has anyone made any moves against you specifically—" she broke off at Sean's look and gazed down at her plate. "Of course you know the drill."

"I also know how to watch my own back."

Jennifer glanced up, then back down at her food. "Don't get touchy on me again. I'm not being confrontational here."

Sean studied her bent head. He *was* being sensitive, but she couldn't know that part of his touchiness had to do with his unexpected reaction to her and not the bad footing that had marked the start of their partnership.

It was more of the same awareness that had hit him the first time he'd really looked at her at Lattimore's house.

Today, her hair was loose. She looked soft and relaxed, not at all like the adversary with the attitude she'd initially presented herself to be. She looked young, too. He had no idea what her age was. Twenty-something? Surely not much older.

"Do I have food on my face?" Jennifer asked, looking up. Then she smiled.

Sean smiled, too, at having been caught staring. "Sorry. I was just thinking, you don't look as if you could have been with the bureau for very long."

Still smiling, Jennifer took a sip of her orange juice, then she set the glass down. "I'm thirty, not twenty. I'm also an ex-Marine, which means I've been around the block more than once. I graduated top in my class at Quantico, and since then few of my older colleagues have had a problem with my relatively short career or youth."

"None who lived to tell about it, I'm sure." Sean picked up his coffee cup.

Jennifer saw the look in his eye and laughed a little at herself. "You're saying I come on sort of strong?"

Sean shrugged, smiling a bit himself. "A little. But then, with that impressive pedigree I guess you're entitled to."

Jennifer leaned back. "So says the pot calling the kettle—" Realizing the unintended pun she'd almost made on a pun, Jennifer caught Sean's eye. They both laughed softly.

"Okay," he said. "So maybe we're both entitled. Tell me about yourself, Jennifer Bennett."

Jennifer looked at him, bemused. Somehow, she hadn't envisioned Sean getting personal enough anywhere in this assignment to field that sort of question.

Because beneath his benign request, she heard the interest of an attracted man, not just a curious colleague.

"I didn't mean to make you uncomfortable," Sean said, noting her hesitation. "You don't have to answer if you don't want to." He took a bite of food and gazed casually around the restaurant.

The other patrons were older couples, young ones with kids, and bustling waitresses in their perky red and white aprons. The place had the feel of a modern-day weigh station. People coming, people going, people just settling down inside the hubbub a while to get out of their houses.

"It's not that," Jennifer finally said. She was unsure how to respond, because she was unsure how she felt about him. She hadn't missed the surreptitious looks other patrons who assumed they were a couple were giving them. She opted to keep it light. "Sometimes, I get a little sensitive to the question because of my background."

"You mean your grandfather, and his friendship with Collins."

Jennifer looked him in the eye. "You're direct, Agent Alexander."

"Am I wrong, or didn't you want it out on the table?"

"It was eventually going to find its way there, wasn't it?"

Sean just shrugged, lifted his coffee cup, took another long sip.

"I've never made any apologies for being close to my grandfather and I never will, no matter how that relationship gets interpreted."

"I'm not asking you to apologize. I was just curious to know. General Gerard Bennett has a reputation as a formidable man."

"Yes, in more ways than you could know. My parents were killed in a plane crash when I was nine. Grandpa never questioned taking me in, even though he was a widower and military man who had for years been living a solitary, regimented life." Jennifer smiled.

She looked unexpectedly winsome, so much so in that moment that Sean smiled, too.

"It was love at first sight for both of us. I thought my world had ended after my parents were gone. I didn't have any siblings, and the fact that Mama was pregnant when she died only made the lack seem worse."

"I'm sorry." And Sean was. Such a heavy tragedy at that tender age was more than anyone should have to bear.

"Thank you," Jennifer said softly, holding his eyes a little longer than she intended. When his stilled just a fraction before shifting back down to his almost empty plate, Jennifer mentally nudged herself.

"In the years that followed, Grandpa spoiled me horribly. Not at the expense of forgetting to teach me lessons that mattered about decency and responsibility, and honor for honor's sake.

"But he had a lot of unchaneled love he'd bottled up inside after his son married and moved away, and his wife died, leaving him too. I've always known there isn't anything he wouldn't do for me, and I feel absolutely the same about him."

Sean leaned forward, resting his elbows on the table and clasping his hands. "He sounds like quite a man, quite a contrast to the blood-and-guts hero he earned himself a reputation for being in Korea."

Relaxed by Sean's inviting tone, Jennifer leaned forward, too, and smiled again in spite of herself. And found herself caught in the hypnotic depth of his eyes. She even imagined she detected a hint of brogue when he spoke, although of course such imagining was pure fancy.

"Oh, Grandpa's no softy, you can believe that," she continued. "Despite the pampering, he rode my butt when I needed it every time I tested him or straddled the line. He can melt me with a look, make no mistake. But he can also pin me with that Gerry Bennett glare that still makes me shake."

"Fear of God, hm?" Sean's smile deepened.

"Hm," Jennifer merely agreed after a pensive moment. A personal and bittersweet addendum to the thought kept her from elaborating.

Sean sensed she had withdrawn a little. He was surprised at how strongly he was tempted to pursue. Whether she knew it or not, Agent Bennett had inherited some of the power of her grandfather's presence. Without even trying, she drew a reluctant man in.

But because he remembered who they were and why they were together, he unclasped his hands and leaned back in his chair.

"So, I think tit for tat is only fair," Jennifer said,

watching his retreat. She ignored a part of her that might have been disappointed, reminding herself of the prudence of letting his caution ride.

"Well, I don't have any famous personages in my pedigree."

"No, you're a famous personage all by yourself."

"You know, that whole thing can get a little tiresome."

Jennifer studied him, trying to figure out if he was being philosophical or if he was annoyed.

Sean looked up to see her watching him, no doubt wanting to pick his brain. The sharpest ones always did. "You just do your job, and hopefully everything keeps coming out for the best," he explained.

"Then tell me what really happened in California, Sean."

Chapter Six

"Mr. Amory, how can I help you today, sir?"

"I need to put in a prescription." Roy handed his doctor's order over the counter to his pharmacist.

The pharmacist read it and looked up. "Would you like to wait on that, or will you pick it up later as usual?"

"Later when I get off work, thanks."

"Did you realize you were on the final refill?"

"Yeah. I hope I won't be needing any more after this one." If things went as he suspected, he surely wouldn't.

The pharmacist smiled. "All right then, sir. Have a good day."

Roy raised a hand in thanks and turned away from the counter. A sale bin of candy bars caught his eye and he impulsively picked up a handful, thinking of Charlie. He walked back to the pharmacist who smiled expectantly.

"Can you ring these up for me?" Roy asked, pulling out his wallet.

"Sure. Got a sweet tooth there, do you?"

"Yeah. Thanks, again." Roy accepted his change and, for the second time, turned to leave. The sealed letter in his pocket he'd drop into the mailbox outside.

It was only an hour later, while he was filling his second prescription of the morning, that the pharmacist realized something odd.

Wasn't it Mr. Amory who came into the pharmacy semipanicked one day less than a month ago to purchase Benadryl for an allergic reaction?

The culprit, he'd explained in irritated distress, had been nuts he hadn't known were in some chicken salad a coworker had brought to work.

So why in the world would the man be buying a whole handful of candy bars full of peanuts for himself now?

"I'm sure you know the facts," Sean said. "I'd been working through a reassignment from Indianapolis to the California office for several months. Then last January, three terrorists posing as parents walked into the Beardsly Elementary School one Saturday morning. The group leader, Albert Brady pulled a pistol on the principal and ordered him to alert the media to certain demands—"

"While his two cohorts positioned themselves inside a classroom. There, they proceeded to hold at gunpoint the teacher and four children who were preparing to leave on a field trip."

"Yes. What I was able to establish with Brady later was that he and his partners wanted the school closed down, not out of some belief that the developmentally challenged children it taught were abominations, as the press erroneously reported.

"Rather, Brady and his gang considered the Beardsly students God's special children, handpicked by the Lord to flourish and touch the world with mystical gifts He had given them and only He understood."

"Brady viewed the Beardsly children as handpicked messengers who—how did he put it?"

"Who carried revelations of truth they would give the world as God directed them. Revelations that were being systematically erased from the children's minds by the school's institutional teaching."

Jennifer shook her head. "Exactly where did Brady want the children to go as an alternative?"

"He wanted them returned to their homes and, as he put it, not interfered with. That way God's purpose would be allowed to shine through as He intended, for the good of mankind."

"And the explosives his gang had literally planted around the base of the school building?"

"Brady was fully prepared to send himself, his partners, and those children back to their maker if the society that imprisoned them didn't listen to him and set them free."

He frowned. "By the morning after the school's seizure, everyone was deeply frustrated. Almost twenty-four hours straight of talking had passed with no progress.

"No one really thought Brady would let those children go. Not the professional hostage negotiators, not the media who continued to broadcast every whisper of the spectacle. Not the parents who had gathered to plead for the lives of their kids. And not me, though I'd been specially assigned to assist the hostage specialists in charge of the negotiation."

As caught up now as she had been when the drama had unfolded originally, Jennifer leaned on the table. She pushed her empty plate aside and folded her hands beside it.

"But you got through to Brady despite all that. How, Sean? I know the actual words you used to persuade him, because of the television cameras. But how did you know *what* to say, what argument would really make him consider releasing those children?"

Sean was remembering that final showdown.

"It was clear enough to everyone outside the school that Brady was ready to snap. The detonation device he held in his hand was clearly one twitchy movement away from being deployed. It was only that wavering millisecond of possibility that kept the marksmen who were brought onto the scene at bay.

"And I knew that even if the shooters could find a way to take Brady out, we had no guarantee the terrorists inside wouldn't blow the school anyway."

"That's when you decided to intervene with the negotiators, to ask them to let you try one more appeal," Jennifer said. "You knew there was nothing to lose and maybe still some time to be bought in an effort to save those lives."

Sean was nodding. "Yes, and they agreed. I gambled. I figured if all their arguments about the value of the children's lives and their own still weren't working, we needed to get more fundamental with Brady. We needed to hit him and his men where they really lived, ideologically speaking.

"It seemed to me that more than the public attention they craved for their cause, more than the children's salvation they claimed to want, they were being motivated by fear. So that was the button I pushed."

Jennifer said, "You told Brady if he snatched those children back from God before God was ready to receive them, he and his cohorts would be the ones going to Hell."

"Yes, and it was no different from the argument the hostage negotiators had already offered really. But I framed it differently, biblically, because I suspected a direct appeal in the literal name of God would reach him. *But Jesus said, Suffer little children, and forbid them not, to come unto me: for of such is the kingdom of heaven.*"

"Yes," Jennifer nodded.

"What Brady heard, of course, was that by harming the children, he was spitting in the face of the God he claimed he and his men were there to serve.

"I was able to make him feel the fear of endangering not only the Beardsly children's lives, but those of all special children like them who hadn't yet been sent by God to Earth. I don't even know why I thought of that bible passage." He laughed a little, but it was a sound of irony.

"What?"

"I was just thinking maybe it's true what they say about Catholics. We can never really stray, no matter how badly we lapse. Or maybe it was just the extreme pressure of the situation. Stress can make unexpected creatures of us all."

"Even would-be heroes."

Sean looked up at Jennifer's pensive tone. Her soft

expression made him uncomfortable and pulled him back where he needed to be.

"Whatever. I only know that my reasoning appeared as if it was going to work. We could all see Brady wavering, actually kneeling down to put the detonator on the ground."

Sean picked up his condensation-covered water glass. Instead of drinking, he stared into it while their waitress cleared away their plates.

After the woman left, Jennifer urged, "What?"

"Brady never said another word, never gave the faintest indication of what he was about to do before he did it. He just detonated those explosives. He took out himself, his partners, the children, and their teacher."

Yes, Jennifer thought soberly. He also took something out of the only man able to reach him that day, an indefinable something whose ravages had been cruelly recorded in the stunned aftermath for a country to see.

While the television cameras rolled, Sean Alexander, clearly more devastated than any of his colleagues believed he'd been justified to be, walked into the smoky rubble of the explosion. He'd said not a word to the hysterical parents, babbling reporters, or shocked school officials around him.

He'd merely stood amidst the debris that used to be the school. Then he'd knelt down to retrieve what glory-seeking photographers would win national awards for. He had plucked out of the devastation a stuffed teddy bear, bloodied and torn. Pressing the toy to his chest, Sean had lifted his face to the God his desolate expression accused of having forsaken the children in His care.

"Afterward, I went through the mandatory bureau counseling. Then I went back to work. But . . . I needed—I wanted a transfer. I was relocated back to Indianapolis." Long moments passed. Sean said nothing more and Jennifer didn't press him. She watched him alternately stare down at the table, then out around the room at the laughing families whose own children had years of life left to live.

Hearing the story from Sean's own lips without any third-party intervention left Jennifer unexpectedly speechless. And more. She was moved by this glimpse of something bigger than any live television camera or radio feed ever could have had the power to convey.

Life unplugged, she supposed. Nothing more and certainly nothing less.

Sean suddenly finished his water. Jennifer was startled to hear all traces of introspection stripped from his voice when he said, "I've already put in a retrieval request at the California field office for the Beardsly case file.

"Included should be not only profiles on the terrorists, but also schematics of the school, the names of the dead, the children's parents and guardians, and the personnel who worked and died there. The faxes should be in my hands by no later than tonight.''

Jennifer let his words dissolve into the bright chattery atmosphere. She still was feeling moved to want to comfort him somehow, or at least to reassure him with words he clearly didn't want to hear.

Because now he was all brusqueness again, all business when he'd been gripped only moments ago by memories of despair.

Well, Jennifer thought, perhaps his attitude was only proper. She, too, had come here to do a job first and foremost, hadn't she? She'd do well to regard Sean's don't-touch-me attitude now a well-timed, unsentimental reminder of that.

She gathered her purse and picked up the bill. ''Are you ready? Emily Marsh should be arriving at her office shortly. We can catch her first thing if we move.''

Sean placed a tip on the table and pushed back his own chair. ''After you,'' he invited.

Jennifer hesitated at the last minute after all, until he looked directly at her, until he met her eyes. She saw in his the lingering hint of shadows his voice and attitude so forcefully belied. Oddly reassured, she walked past him out into the aisle.

*   *   *

O'Brien's assessment was that Milo's Furniture and Collectibles, nice as it was, specialized in the kind of merchandise he wouldn't have favored even if he and his wife could have afforded it.

Obvious and, to his way of thinking, ostentatious pieces no doubt saddled with names like Hepplewhite and Chippendale dominated here with only minor exceptions. He glanced at Clemm and could tell that even though he tried to appear relaxed, he was wary of breaking and, therefore, touching. Clemm did pick up a price tag once, glance at it, and drop it quickly.

O'Brien suppressed a smile. He focused instead on the smartly dressed woman briskly threading her way through cleverly arranged sofa and chair groupings to meet them.

"Gentlemen, I'm Marta Blaine, the owner here. Can I help you with something?"

O'Brien pulled out his identification and shield and flashed them for Ms. Blaine to see. Her expression took on the slightly tense, eager-to-please look civilians usually acquired when faced with the famous credentials. The law-abiding ones, that was.

O'Brien said, "Ms. Blaine, thank you for agreeing to meet with us this morning." He caught the eye of another sales attendant who was trying to look as if he weren't hanging on every word. "Perhaps we could go to your office."

"Of course. Please, follow me. Can I offer you coffee? It's freshly brewed. Maybe cappuccino?"

"No thanks, ma'am, I'm fine."

Clemm concurred.

Marta Blaine's office managed to look functional, yet also as hands-off-unless-you-intend-to-buy as her showroom. She settled herself behind a wide desk O'Brien was sure carried one of those designer names.

He also decided clutter was too indelicate a term for the papers scattered atop it. Genteel disarray seemed more fitting for the files, notepads, gold pen, and calculator sitting there.

Blaine told them, "I've already pulled the file I think you'll be interested in."

Clemm half rose from his chair and leaned over her desk to accept it.

She explained, "It's the file of our former manager, Ben Keaghan. He was in charge of operations almost up until the time period you're interested in. He would have been in charge of controller operations, well, at least in seeing that the new person was in place to carry them out following his departure."

"Was he fired, ma'am?" Clemm asked.

"No, he handed in his two weeks notice about four weeks ago. His employment actually ended one week ago. That's when the new manager, whom you may have seen out on the floor, took over his duties."

"But Keaghan was here when Lattimore bought the furniture that—" O'Brien checked the file Clemm had passed to him—"John Paine and Jimmy Martins were assigned to deliver?"

"That's right."

"And he left before that assignment was actually confirmed?"

"Yes. The new man actually logged the assignment in. Mr. Keaghan simply gave him the instructions of how he should do that when the time came."

"Ms. Blaine, why did Mr. Keaghan leave? Was he dissatisfied with his job here?"

"On the contrary. In fact, he apologized for resigning. But he said the fact was, he felt he was neglecting aspects of his other career, which was more vital to him."

"And that career is?"

"Mr. Keaghan is an artist."

"A painter?" O'Brien ignored Marta Blaine's delicate wince at what she apparently thought should have been a loftier characterization.

"Not that sort of artist, Agent O'Brien. His medium was wood."

Something niggled in O'Brien's mind. But Blaine was still talking.

"He was in the process of trying to make a local reputation for himself as a carver and designer."

The cabin. In the vicinity of the crime scene. Mauer had told him one of the occupants was a woodcarver. Coincidence? Maybe not. "You say he left your employment exactly one week ago?"

"Yes. Is that odd? I can assure you Ben was a model employee. I wish he was still with us."

"And he had no occasion to visit the premises after he left? To the best of your knowledge?"

"Well, no. Here, let me call Harry to confirm that." Marta Blaine punched a button on her intercom phone. An answering voice provided a muffled response.

"Harry, could you step in here a moment, please? No, nothing's wrong, I've just got a question for you. Thanks." Marta Blaine leaned back against her chair, a worried frown creasing her smooth brow.

Her office door opened a crack and the man O'Brien had noticed outside popped his head inside.

"It's all right Harry, come in," his boss directed.

The older man did so, clearly cautious. "Yes, ma'am?"

"Agents?" Blaine motioned for them to ask their questions.

Harry leaned against the wall and clasped his hands in front of him.

O'Brien said, "Sir, we have just a couple of questions about the employee you replaced here, Mr. Ben Keaghan."

"Yes, what about Ben?"

"We understand his term of employment ended one week ago, but that he trained you to take over his job for an extended period prior to that."

"That's right, he did."

"After you actually began working here, did Mr. Keaghan ever visit the store? Perhaps to pick up belongings he'd forgotten."

"Or just to see how you were getting along?" Clemm suggested.

Harry was shaking his head. "No, he didn't. He did call once though, to check up on me exactly as you say."

"And what did you tell him?"

Harry looked at his boss, who gazed calmly back. He shrugged. "I assured him everything was going fine." He threw another glance at Marta Blaine. "It was."

O'Brien said, "During that conversation, did Mr. Keaghan seem curious about any aspect of the business you'd taken over? Were there any customers or accounts in particular he still expressed interest in? Anything at all?"

"Well, there was one outstanding order he knew was going to fall to me to complete and he asked about that. But I didn't consider it unusual because he was just conscientiously following up. That sort of attention to detail was typical of him."

"Yes it was," Marta Blaine commented.

"What was the order?" O'Brien asked.

"It was for the Lattimore account. The details of the delivery had yet to be logged in and finalized before he left. He'd explained the procedure to me so that I'd know how to handle it when the time came. Considering the importance of the customer, Ben wanted to make sure everything was arranged smoothly."

"But he never physically came back on the premises to check it out."

A little miffed, Harry said, "As I told you, gentlemen, I had it under control."

"Can you tell us how you scheduled that order."

"Of course. When Mr. Lattimore was in the store in late September to make the purchase, he requested delivery of the sofa he'd bought. He told us then that he wasn't going to actually be in residence at the house where the piece was to be delivered until early October. That's why he wanted us to wait until later to firm up the delivery plans."

"Okay. What happened next?"

"Well, there's a routine delivery invoice the store fills out. It lists the merchandise, the date of purchase, and date of delivery. The time of delivery is noted, of course, and the names of the drivers to make the run."

"You have a copy of Lattimore's invoice?"

"Of course."

"We'd like a copy of it before we leave."

"Yes, sir."

"Please, go on."

"Well, there's not much more. The invoice information is logged into our computerized data bank, as well as in a written ledger. We're trying to get rid of the ledger system. But since none of us here are tech-heads, that process takes time."

Clemm smiled at the colloquial description that seemed incongruous with the prim little man.

Harry smiled back at Clemm, perhaps finding the younger man's demeanor less intimidating than O'Brien's steady gaze.

Clemm glanced at O'Brien, who nodded slightly. Turning his attention back to Harry, Clemm said, "Did anything unusual, I mean out of the ordinary in the course of daily business, occur after Mr. Keaghan left?"

"Well," Harry looked at Marta Blaine, who was leaning forward.

"Yes, gentlemen, in fact it did," she said.

Clemm waited.

"One week ago from yesterday, my store was robbed."

O'Brien and Clemm looked at each other.

"Harry, you can leave now, thank you very much," Marta Blaine said. "And please shut the door behind you." Harry backed out of the room.

"What was taken, Ms. Blaine?" O'Brien asked.

"Well, it was all very odd. You see, apparently, nothing was taken. There was some disruption to the floor, furniture overturned, displays pulled out of alignment. A couple of sofas were slashed, as if to make it *seem* as if things had been stolen. But a careful inventory check showed that nothing was actually stolen."

Clemm met O'Brien's eyes again, then said to Blaine, "And the police weren't successful in turning up any suspects?"

"No. That is, they haven't yet. But the case is still open. The police tell me sometimes the motive for break-ins isn't always theft. Sometimes, the objective is vandalism, and they speculate that's what happened here. Just some kids maybe breaking into a store for kicks."

"What about your office, and your manager's office? Any damage in either one?"

"Not at all. In fact, the doors to both offices were still locked the morning I arrived and discovered the mess."

O'Brien said, "We'd like to amend our request for

that Lattimore invoice. Instead of a copy, we'd like to take the original with us."

"You think this robbery could be connected?"

"We really can't say that, ma'am."

"But I don't understand. Harry explained to you that he's the only one who handled the invoice. Surely, you don't suspect Harry of any wrongdoing?"

"We have no reason to."

O'Brien glanced at Clemm and saw by his expression that he was on the same page.

An ex-employee showed a lingering interest in a customer whose son just happened to be kidnapped shortly after that employee's virtual disappearance? That same ex-employee voiced his love of a wood-carving avocation, and a woodcarver just happened to live near Lattimore's country home. A robbery in which nothing was stolen; indeed, in which the two sources of ready cash—two locked offices—were the only things in the store left undisturbed.

A customer invoice that was the only documentation detailing not only the time Lattimore's delivery was to be made, but also the delivery men and the route they were to take.

A collection of coincidences? Possible, O'Brien thought. But his stronger feeling was, not.

"Sheriff, we have something." Mauer punched up the volume on his radio. He was just getting back to the woods after sharing a light breakfast with his wife at home.

He'd been solemn company for her. And though she didn't ask, she'd been a cop's wife too long not to suspect the lack of progress on the search in the woods was getting to him.

Mauer had appreciated her not pressing him on it, because he couldn't deny his frustration. It had lasted during the ride all the way back here to the site. Now, one of his deputies was sounding hopeful.

Mauer parked his car at the side of the road and started up the incline, where his deputy met him.

"What did you find, Dave?"

"A grave, sir."

Well, shit, Mauer thought. "Where is it?"

"Not two miles southeast of here." The deputy pointed. "Over by the Little Wilky River. The boys are still digging, but the early signs—"

"Yeah?"

"It looks like a double one, sir."

Chapter Seven

Charlie sat up, abruptly pulled from sleep. Had someone called him? His mother? Or was it the lady who had tricked him, pretending to be his mother? No, she had disappeared. Maybe the man had killed her. Maybe she was dead now, too.

Or maybe he'd just heard her in his dream.

In his dream, his mother *had* come to him again, telling him to wake up. He'd cried because he couldn't.

He raised a hand to his cheek now, feeling the dream tears still on his face.

In the dream, his mother had told him what to do. He couldn't stay asleep. He needed to start helping himself. He sat on the edge of the bed now, still a little fuzzy, and shook his head to clear it. Then reached for the switch on the lamp, as the man had done.

Dim light lit the floor around his bed, leaving the

greater area of the basement room dark. Didn't matter. He could see well enough.

Well enough to search these walls for his window.

He hopped off the bed, tilting his wrist so that he could see his watch. Still morning. The man was at work. Plenty of time to look.

Sean punched on the car phone. "Yeah?"

"Mauer here. We found something, a grave with two bodies in it. My guess is they're the delivery men. The coroner is examining them now. I'm also guessing the bullets in their necks will provide our thirty-eight-caliber match."

"Anything else?"

"The boys are still searching. The bodies were nude, so whoever killed them probably used their uniforms in order to get past Lattimore's security."

"Bennett and I are on our way to interview Marsh. If our luck holds, we'll collect a few more pieces to this."

"Right."

"Keep in touch." Sean replaced the phone, saying to Jennifer, "Maurer's people found two bodies. Odds are they're the real Milo boys."

Emily Marsh was younger than Jennifer had expected. Early thirties, she guessed. But the concern in her eyes and eagerness to help seemed genuine as she ushered them past her receptionist and into her therapy den.

That's how the atmosphere of the office struck Jennifer—like that of a den. Nothing overtly functional here. Only the cushiest furniture. Emily Marsh's desk was small, unobtrusive, and flanked by a rolltop desk that served as her credenza. To the side of that, beneath the massive office window that dominated the room, was a series of built-in bookcases.

They housed what Jennifer supposed were auxiliary tools of the therapist's trade. Stuffed animals, rag dolls, board games, puzzles. Even a small television topped by a video cassette recorder. Arrayed beside that was a series of kid's videos. Disney, visible on the spines of many of them, seemed the dominant theme.

"How can I help you?" Emily Marsh said, settling herself behind her desk and coming straight to the point.

Sean answered. "As I explained over the phone, we'd like some detailed background information about Charlie Lattimore."

"The sort that only his shrink can provide, hm?"

Jennifer frowned, wondering at the doctor's hesitation.

Sean assessed the doctor, too. "That's right. We need to know more about his frame of mind right before his mother's death, and in the wake of it."

"Well you know I can't discuss certain facts with you because of patient confidentiality. I'm afraid some things will have to remain confidential."

"Wrong, Ms. Marsh," Jennifer said. "We're talking about a kidnapping here, about a little boy's life, which may end in three days if we don't get to him before his abductor decides to kill him. That changes the rules and blows your confidentiality restriction to hell. Do *you* understand?"

Emily Marsh looked at Sean. He just gazed back, offering her nothing. Then he said, "So, let's begin again. Tell us about Charlie's therapy. How often did he see you? How were his sessions structured? How were the records of those sessions kept?"

Emily Marsh started to answer, then seemingly thought better of it and got up to pace. She stood at her window, her back to the room. "You have to understand something, first. I didn't mean to be difficult a moment ago. It's just that, I love that little boy. I was friends with his mother before she died, and I wasn't unaware of the problems in their home before Cheryl got sick.

"I apologize. Certainly, I'll help you in any way I can."

Jennifer looked at Sean. The remembered admonition from Paul Lattimore to go easy on her hovered between them.

Sean turned back to Marsh. "Paul Lattimore has

already explained to us Charlie's difficulty in coping with his mother's death. He says before she died, she and Charlie shared an unusually strong bond. One of their favorite things to do was spend time in the gazebo that adjoins the Lattimore country house."

"Yes, that's right," Emily Marsh confirmed.

"As far as you know, is she the only one Charlie spent time with there?"

"Well, yes. When she wasn't with him, he sometimes liked to go there alone."

"Did he ever talk about going there with his father?"

"No."

Jennifer's brow rose at the clipped response. "Why not?" she asked.

Now the therapist turned to face them. She leaned back against the sill, bracing her weight on her hands. "You should understand something about a period in the relationship between Charlie Lattimore and his mother and father. After they first moved here from Washington, the family dynamic was . . . strained. According to Cheryl, she and Paul were having problems, and as kids do, Charlie picked up on that.

"I had some early conversations with Paul and he admitted going through a period of extreme stress. You can imagine—his wife's health, his abrupt career change, leaving behind the energy of the national spotlight. The gazebo was conceived as an after-thought to the retreat, built at Cheryl's request.

"Despite their problems, Paul Lattimore loved his wife and tried to do for her whatever she asked. He thought building her a place of her own, as she wanted, would demonstrate that fact."

"And did Cheryl Lattimore view it that way?"

"Not at first. She was struggling with her fear of the cancer and with a certainty—erroneous, I might add—that Paul didn't love her, that he was looking for ways to avoid her. She even spoke to me of divorce, said she would have pursued it with Paul had not concern for Charlie held her back."

"She wanted to keep the family together, despite her problems with Paul," Sean said.

"Yes, Mr. Alexander, that's correct. Instead of drawing them closer together, the gazebo became a symbol of their inability to bridge their difficulties. Charlie fell into the habit of accompanying Cheryl there, then took that habit further by elevating its importance as their special place."

"And Paul?" Sean asked.

"Paul was devastated. But he felt openly raising an objection to that bond between his son and wife would just strain an already tough situation. I advised him that, no matter what the relationship was between him and Cheryl, Charlie didn't doubt his love. I advised him to hold onto that. If Charlie seemed to be favoring one parent over the other, it was only because he knew how sick his mother was. He was sensitive to her depression and, in a child's way, stuck closer to her as his way of helping her cope with that."

Sean said, "Everything you're telling us now came out in your sessions with Charlie?"

"Mostly, yes."

"And how did you record those sessions?"

"I tape-record my sessions with all my patients. Charlie's were no exception."

"And where do you keep the tapes?"

Marsh hesitated. "Is this where you ask me to turn them over to the federal authorities for scrutiny?"

"Is this where you object?"

Emily Marsh held his stare, then deflated. "Like I said, I want to cooperate. I kept two sets of Charlie's tapes. Before you ask, there's nothing unusual in that. I keep dual sets on all my patients, one for here, and the other for home. I'm often up late into the night, reviewing facts."

"Who has access to your tapes here at the office?"

"No one. I keep them under strict lock and key. There's only one key, and I maintain control of that."

"You mean you have that key in your possession all the time."

"Yes. I wouldn't leave something that important lying around on my desk or anywhere else somebody could get to it. In Charlie's case, as with my other patients, I never made an exception to that rule.''

''Never? You didn't forget one day for an hour, maybe two, and then retrieve the key from where you'd left it later.''

''Not a chance.''

''What about the other set of tapes. The ones at your home?''

''What about them? Specifically?''

''Were you as meticulous about preserving their security there, in surroundings that were less guarded, more relaxed?'' Jennifer asked.

''Absolutely. I keep them in a safe.''

''Where inside your house is your safe?''

''In my study. It's secured by a combination lock, not by a lock and key.''

Sean said, ''And of course you haven't shared the combination with anyone.''

Emily Marsh hesitated.

''Have you?'' he pressed.

''It's just,'' she sighed, ''I had a new safe recently installed. A few months ago, I decided to update it to something more state-of-the-art. The combination changed. For about two weeks, I kept the numbers written down in a small notebook I use to jot down miscellaneous notes to myself. No one would have any reason to look inside it.''

"Are you saying there were times when someone *could* have gotten a look at your notebook?"

Marsh sighed again. "I came home a couple of times to discover I'd gone into the book for some other information, and had forgotten to lock it away in my desk drawer. I'd left it on my blotter. I have no reason to suspect, however, that it was disturbed either of those times."

"But if it could have been, who could have done it? Do you live alone?"

"Yes."

"Did you have any houseguests during those times who the book could have been exposed to?"

"Friends came over occasionally, but no one who was ever in the house while I wasn't."

"What about anyone who had access to enter the house while you weren't inside it?"

"The only one who has a house key is the woman I use from a cleaning service twice a week. I hardly think she's a candidate."

"Why not?" Jennifer asked.

"Well, if you met Judy, you'd understand. She's hardly the type to display much interest in anything besides the details of her job."

Why you're a snob, Jennifer thought. "But she *did* have a house key?"

"Well, I've already said that. Yes."

"On what days of the week does Judy come to clean?"

"Well that's hardly relevant now. She quit."

Sean looked at Jennifer. To Marsh, he said, "When?"

"Last week. I didn't see anything unusual in it, people in that sort of vocation usually come and go. Their services are easily replaced, and I replaced Judy."

"Have you had any reason between her departure and now to check on the status of the tapes in your safe? Charlie's in particular?"

"Unusually enough, no. My evenings haven't been as long, lately. Besides that, Charlie's sessions have dwindled off considerably within the last year. For him, there just haven't been that many new tapes."

Jennifer asked, "So when was the last time you checked your safe at home, doctor?"

Marsh looked from one to the other, making a disbelieving sound. "Oh, come on. Are you really suggesting my housekeeper somehow knew to search my day book for a combination buried among a zillion other facts—a book that was only left in sight for limited snatches of time—and then used that knowledge to break into my safe?"

Jennifer and Sean said nothing.

"That's ridiculous."

But Jennifer thought she suddenly sounded a little

less certain. "I think Agent Alexander would agree that perhaps it would be worth our while to take a drive to your house."

Marsh looked incredulous. "What, do you mean now? I have patients coming."

"I'd suggest you consider rescheduling," Sean said.

Sean and Jennifer stood beside Emily Marsh, waiting for her to finish entering the combination to her private safe. When she opened it, she reached inside and withdrew a wide leather case that probably had been originally designed to store music cassettes. She set the case down on the desk behind her and unsnapped the strap that secured it.

A few seconds into her check, she went very still. "Oh my God," she whispered.

Jennifer stepped forward.

Emily Marsh looked up. The color in her face had noticeably paled. "His tapes are missing. Charlie's tapes are missing. I can't *believe* this!"

Sean said, "Perhaps you'd better give us Judy's full name and her cleaning service's address and phone number."

"Jane Doe is crashing!"

"*Shit*. Sorry," the doctor added belatedly, making her apologies to the wide-eyed parents of a child whose broken arm she had just set. She ran from the waiting room for the intensive care unit where the crisis was occurring.

"What are her vital signs?" she demanded from the intern commandeering the crash cart beside her.

"Her blood pressure is dangerously low and falling. Respiration is erratic. Her pulse is spotty, and she's going into cardiac arrest."

They pushed through the unit doors into the room. A nurse was at the woman's bedside, leaning low over her ominously still form.

"Move out of the way!" the doctor demanded, "I need to get at her."

"No, wait, she's trying to say something," the nurse insisted, excited.

"She won't be saying *anything* if you don't get the hell out of the way." The doctor shoved the woman aside.

Then suddenly, she, the nurse, and the other attendants in the room were stunned when Jane Doe sat up with an unnatural burst of strength.

"Hell," her stunned doctor sputtered, "let's restrain her, people, *now!*"

"Hal? Where's Hal?" Judy gasped. With her already dwindling strength, she managed to open her eyes very slightly. She registered intent expressions on the faces of the white-coated people standing around her. Then someone was trying to push her down. *No!* She had to make them understand. "Hal!"

The doctor watched Jane Doe fall back to the mattress. The energy that had so startlingly infused her seeped completely away, leaving her as limp as a rag doll. The doctor didn't wait for more miracles, she went to work.

"Falling . . . her pressure is falling . . ." Judy heard from a distance. *I'm sorry I involved you, Hal. You too, Ben. But I loved him. I still love him . . .*

She couldn't hold onto that thought . . . any thought . . . any longer. Everything was going dark. *I'm sorry, Hal. Sorry . . .*

"Who's Hal?" the nurse asked.

"Doesn't matter, he'll never see her alive again," the doctor answered. She stripped off her vinyl gloves as she stepped back from the bed and the still figure upon it.

And all of a sudden, the doctor remembered the other time Jane Doe had spoken. She hadn't been saying "how." She'd been saying *"Hal."* She'd been asking for someone named Hal.

"Mary," the doctor directed the nurse, "I want you to go back to the floor station and get a message through to that FBI agent, Bob Clemm. He left his number there."

"Are you sure, Doctor?"

The doctor backed away from the bed and met her

other colleagues' sober looks. "Absolutely sure. I'm calling time of death." She looked at the clock on the wall above the bed. "Twelve noon."

"Is the name Hal all you were able to get?"

"Yes, Agent Clemm. I'm only sorry we couldn't understand her earlier. Maybe we could have found him for her."

"Don't sweat it, you did all you could." Bob Clemm hung up the phone and stepped outside the shelter of the roadside phone booth from which he'd answered his page. Back inside the car, he told O'Brien, "Jane Doe is dead."

O'Brien grimaced. "Well, why not. If she'd lived, that would have made things too easy for us."

"As it turns out, all might not be lost. She said something before she went. A name. Somebody named Hal. Maybe *he*, whoever he is, can do the trick for us."

"Maybe. Let's call Sean."

"Excuse me, Doctor?"

The doctor turned to see a tall, dark, burly man circumventing people in the busy hallway outside the intensive care unit to reach her. The determined look on his face and the timing of his appearance gave her an odd feeling.

When he reached her, she impulsively asked, "Is your name Hal?"

"What?" the man said, startled. "No."

"Oh, I'm sorry. I thought—"

"But I'm here to see a patient of yours." How the hell had she known about Hal? "A burn victim, the one they found by that abandoned truck?" He planted himself in front her and crossed his brawny arms over his wide chest.

The doctor regrouped, though the strange feeling persisted. "Do you know her? Are you family?"

"Yeah, I know Judy. Can I see her?"

"Judy—?"

"Can I *see* her?"

The doctor took an involuntary step back. Something about this man spelled violence. She tried to surreptitiously catch the eye of a security guard who was flirting with one of the young LPNs at the nurses station. The guard never looked up. But the man before her was watching her closely. His eyes narrowed. "Well?" he demanded.

"I'm sorry to have to tell you this, Mr.—?"

He didn't help her.

"Your friend, Judy, just died about five minutes ago."

He dropped his arms and looked past the young doctor at the room he imagined she'd just come out of.

The doctor watched his reaction, the fixed look on his face. "I'm sorry." Impulsively, she extended a comforting hand toward him.

He ducked the touch, stepped back with a muttered, "Thanks," and turned on his heel to walk away.

The doctor watched him go, taking note of the creased denim jeans, the blue plaid flannel shirt. The Nike tennis shoes he wore. His height, approximate weight, the way he wore his hair short on the top and sides, long in the back.

Details she had no doubt Bob Clemm would later appreciate.

Ben Keaghan lit a cigarette in the parking lot. He let the warm sun beat down on him while he leaned against his truck and smoked. And heard the doctor telling him again, "Your friend, Judy, just died . . ."

Roy, you cocksucker son-of-a-bitch. You're dead. Dead!

Chapter Eight

"Yeah, Bob, thanks." Sean placed the phone receiver back on his console and looked up at Jennifer, who was sitting across from his desk. "The bad news is, Jane Doe just died. However, we have a partial name for her. Judy."

"Judy? It can't be—"

"Sometimes, Agent Bennett, you get lucky." He turned his chair a little and looked over his shoulder. "Arty! What did we get on Emily Marsh's info?"

A short, slender young agent in white shirtsleeves walked across the room. He carried a computer print-out with him.

"Her full name is Judy Keaghan. Age thirty-two. For the last year, she worked as a domestic in a variety of odd jobs before landing a position with the cleaning service Marsh contracted her from."

"And before that?" Jennifer asked.

"She was a nurse, a registered one."

"Where did she work?"

"In a public health clinic close to where Charlie Lattimore was snatched."

"So how did she fall from professional to domestic?"

"Accusations of professional impropriety. Her clinic was coming off some local press about alleged patient care violations. My guess is, when the questions about Keaghan came up, they probably didn't want the additional mess of calling her out publicly. So, they seem to have paid her a nice severance package to just go away."

"Which was where?"

"Her last recorded address is in the wilds of Southern Indiana. It's false, though, there's no residence there. We'll keep working on it."

"Sean, line two."

Sean raised a hand to acknowledge the agent holding the call for him.

Jennifer watched him take the call. He lounged comfortably in his chair, his long powerful body relaxed and at ease. In fact, this was the first time since she'd met him that Special Agent-in-Charge Sean Alexander didn't look tense. He was entirely in his element and, at this moment, fully in charge.

"Paul, yeah. There have been some developments." Sean listened a minute, his body going still.

Jennifer leaned forward, picking up on his intensity.

"Do you have it in front of you now? Okay, read it to me."

Sensing something breaking, more agents gathered at Sean's desk. He didn't acknowledge them, but continued to stare down at his desk blotter, his brow creased in concentration. Then he picked up a pen and pulled a pad of paper toward him.

"Give me the spelling." He started to write.

Reading what he was printing upside down, Jennifer made out the name Olin, first name Sidney. It didn't ring a bell. She looked up at the small group that had gathered. They were reading it, too. Their reactions didn't seem any more informed than hers.

"All right, now calm down, Paul. You've got a fax machine there in your office, right? Here's the fax number for the office here. Send it to me. I know it's hard, but don't panic. Just sit tight and wait for our call." He hung up and finally looked at the group around him.

"What?" Jennifer asked for them all.

"Paul just got a letter in the mail. A copy of it should be coming any minute. It's a threat. A former staffer he tangled with in the past apparently sent it. He says he doesn't like Paul's politics anymore now than he did then. He taunts him about having done something about it to finally get Paul's attention."

The agents parted, making way for the one who

had produced the news about Judy Keaghan. He had something else to tell.

"I caught that name you wrote down and did a quick check. He could be a live one, guys. Four months ago, he was arrested on a molestation charge. The alleged victim was a six-year-old neighbor boy."

Jennifer was already on her feet by the time Sean pushed away from his desk. He shrugged on his jacket, concealing his shoulder holster and the pistol it housed. "You got an address on him?"

"Yeah." He stated a location on the outskirts of the city. "Do we go in with backup?"

Every eye turned to Sean. After a moment, he shook his head. "It's premature. This is just a follow-up. We don't have sufficient probable cause yet to do more at this point. For all we know that letter may have been sent by someone other than Olin."

"Or not." Jennifer's voice was hard.

Sean ignored her. Hot headed action would only complicate the situation while facts were so unclear. "Stand by, everybody. If something looks likely to break, we'll call for that backup in plenty of time. Come on," he told Jennifer.

They paused only long enough to snatch the copy of Lattimore's letter Sean ripped off the fax machine.

Sean watched Jennifer while he knocked on Olin's door. Her expression was still stern. She'd barely spoken during the entire drive over. That was, after she'd reiterated how she thought they were making a mistake to approach Olin alone.

"This isn't the O.K. Corral, Bennett," he'd simply said tersely. Now they both stood on the ramshackle porch of a shabby house with dirt roads flanking it, front and back. A dingy shed around the side of the house was just visible to them.

The door opened. A tall man, about mid-thirties, with greasy unkempt dark hair, a threadbare bathrobe over a dull T-shirt, and sneakered feet stood blocking the door. "Yeah, what do you want?"

"FBI," Sean answered, pulling his ID and shield. Jennifer did the same while Sean shouldered the man aside.

"Hey, you can't just come in here!" Olin stood with his back to the still open door. His eyes shifted from Sean to Jennifer, then briefly past them across the room.

Angry, Jennifer assessed. But also tense. She caught Sean's eye and could tell he thought the same. His voice, though, was calm. "We *can* come in, Mr. Olin, when we have reason to believe you may be involved in a federal offense."

Olin blinked. "What offense?"

"Kidnapping." Jennifer said.

He shut his front door. "Who do you think I took?"

"Did you send this to Paul Lattimore?" Sean handed Olin the faxed letter.

Olin read it, handed it back. "Who says I did? Somebody playing a joke on both Lattimore and me?"

Jennifer stepped close to Olin. He took a step back. "Is that what you're saying this is, Sidney? A joke? You didn't mail this letter?"

"Sending mail isn't against the law."

"Implying threat of a federal offense is," Sean answered. "Why did you do it?" Just then, he caught movement out of the corner of his eye, in the shadows of a hall behind Jennifer. He said, "Agent Bennett, see if you can get anything out of him other than this smart talk. Sidney, where's your can?"

Sidney Olin looked disconcerted, then amused. "Over there." He pointed beyond Sean's right shoulder.

Sean looked at Jennifer, moved his head almost imperceptibly, then walked into the bathroom and shut the door.

Jennifer interpreted Sean's warning as one to go easy on the man. She wasn't buying that approach.

"Listen to me, Olin. We know you're not a stupid man, which means you must be a crafty one. You sent that letter to Lattimore to frighten him. What did he do, fire you?"

Olin walked over to a coffee table to pick up a half-full shot glass. He threw back more of what he'd been drinking. "Yeah, he fired me."

"So you took his boy to get him back for humiliating you?"

"I didn't take his kid. That was just talk."

"It wasn't just talk when the police arrested you a few months ago for cornering a six-year-old in the alley behind your house, was it?"

The glass stopped halfway to Olin's mouth, then he emptied it. "That kid lied. His parents dropped the charge, didn't they?"

"With a little intimidation from you?" Just then through the open dining room window, a faint echo of a keening sound drifted across the backyard and into the house. Jennifer knew it had come from the shed. She looked at Olin. He was beginning to look nervous again.

Sean pulled his cell phone from inside his jacket pocket and punched through a call. Somebody was in the back of the house and holding off on the backup had just ceased being an option.

He guessed there also was something in that shed out back that Sidney Olin didn't want them to see.

"Police dispatch," he heard on the line, and proceeded to identify himself. After the request had been noted, Sean tucked the phone back under his jacket. The sound of Jennifer and Olin's voices had ceased.

He leaned down to flush the toilet. What was Jennifer doing?

Jennifer's gun was pressed to Sidney Olin's back. Her other hand was on his arm as she propelled him toward the rear of the house to the back door.

"You can't do this!" he insisted.

"Just move."

Olin had the screen door opened and one foot on the porch by the time the other gun Jennifer never saw took a bead on her back.

Sean opened the bathroom door to an empty living room. A glance out of the open dining room window revealed Jennifer marching a protesting Olin to that shed. *Goddammit*, what was she doing?

He half expected to hear gunshots from the shooter concealed inside the house. He braced for them all the way to the front door.

When they didn't come, he quietly eased through the door, then off the side of the front porch to double around back.

"Open it," Jennifer ordered.

Sidney Olin jerked out of her grip. "You open it."

Jennifer eyed his crossed arms, his belligerent stance, his ridiculous clothes, and his wounded pride. She shifted her pistol to a steadier two-handed grip, keeping the barrel pointed at the shed lock. Her finger was actually pulling the trigger when she heard Sean shout, "Get *down! Gun!*"

She hit the dirt as all hell broke loose.

The bullet that nearly took off her head punched through the shed door centimeters above her. Sidney Olin, who had hit the ground with her, suddenly came at her.

She jabbed her foot out in a solid roundhouse kick, knocking him off his hands and knees, making him suck in air from the impact she inflicted on his upper chest.

Another shot rang out behind her. Time slowed as she turned her head to see Sean grappling on the back porch with a bare-chested, jean-clad man who had materialized from nowhere. The two went down just as she felt Olin's hand touch her leg.

"Bitch!" he gasped, his face twisted with pain and fury. This time, she struck him on the side of the head with her gun. When he jerked and fell back, she knew he wasn't going to get back up.

She was on her feet by the time Sean stood up with his pistol in his hand. He had it pointed at his adversary's back.

"Put your hands behind your neck, *now*!" Sean ordered.

Jennifer watched the man comply.

Her would-be assailant's rifle clattered down the steps and skidded to rest in the dirt.

Sean threw an angry look her way as the first sirens became audible in the distance.

Breathing erratically as much from adrenaline as exertion, Jennifer turned to the shed and took aim again at the padlock. A uniformed patrolman ran around the side of the house just as she squeezed off a shot. The lock shattered.

And Jennifer stood incredulous at what the door sagged open to reveal.

Oh *shit*, she thought. And let her gun drop to her side.

A pack of ill-kept hounds, collectively chained to a stake in the middle of the shed, barked in annoyance. Or in welcome, she thought struck by the absurdity. Suddenly Sidney Olin moaned.

"My dogs! Don't take my dogs."

"Your *stolen* dogs you mean, Sidney," the patrolman said, coming up beside Jennifer. "I thought you promised to stay out of the hunting business?"

Jennifer put her gun back in the holster she wore beneath her light jacket. She ignored the disdainful look she felt the patrolman toss her way. Then she turned, looking for Sean.

He was letting two patrolmen put the shooter on the porch into custody. Then he was striding across the yard at a deceptively casual pace, right at her. When he reached her, he spared her a glance before he cut his eyes to the watching cop. "Officer, I presume you have everything in hand here?"

"Yes." The patrolman gave Sean an ironic smile. Sean returned it with a brief one of his own. But Jennifer could see that tick of Sean's mouth hadn't connected with his eyes. Sighing inwardly, she proceeded him out of the yard and down to where their car was parked.

When they were headed back to the field office, Jennifer turned to him.

"Don't even say anything," he anticipated her. "Just listen to me and hear what I'm telling you."

Hating being chastised like a child, especially when maybe she partially deserved it, Jennifer fumed.

"If you *ever* disobey me like that again, if you ever jeopardize not only your own life, but the lives of any civilians who may be in the line of fire, I'll have your butt. I'll have it not only removed from this case, but nailed to the nearest wall I can find."

"Don't you—"

"Shut up! A goddamned rookie agent wouldn't have been stupid enough to do what you did back there. It's not even the stupidity that pisses me off as much as the danger you put yourself, me, those men, and God knows who else in for the sake of what you thought was going to be *your* big moment. If Charlie Lattimore was in that shed, the proper way to retrieve him was with backup firmly in place. You know that!"

"What I know is that neither of us can honestly say the situation wouldn't have escalated too soon for backup to matter if Charlie Lattimore *had* been inside that shed!"

Sean still angry, answered, "So you decided to single-handedly save the day. Let me tell you something. Lone wolves are only sexy in action novels, babe. In real life they tend to get their asses killed."

Jennifer fell silent, too furious to say more.

So did Sean.

And in silence, each continued to hold stubbornly to their takes on what had happened, and on what *could* have happened. In silence, each reluctantly acknowledged that maybe, just maybe, the other had a valid point.

The celluar beeped. Sean grabbed it. "Yeah?"

"The phones are ringing off the hook, here. Tell me what the media is saying just happened didn't."

Sean let the community relations officer back at the field office hang while he debated. Then he just sighed.

*   *   *

Roy listened to the news break on the radio somebody had turned on inside a cubicle down the line
from his. The engineer the radio belonged to raised
the volume a little as the unbelievable narrative
continued.

*". . . Sidney Olin, thirty-six, has been taken to the
hospital for treatment of minor injuries. The FBI has issued a statement saying everything possible is continuing
to be done to recover Senator Paul Lattimore's son . . ."*

When somebody near the cubicle mentioned the
dogs again, Roy heard more than a few chuckles up
and down the line of his fellow computer technicians.
He smiled slightly because that part *was* funny. Especially when you considered Alexander had to be
ready to spit nails.

*". . . In other developments, the woman rescued at the
site of the abandoned delivery truck believed to have been
involved with the Lattimore kidnapping has been tenta-
tively identified as Judy Keaghan, a thirty-two-year-old
former nurse from Morgan County . . ."*

Roy's heart nearly stopped. He hit an erroneous
button on his keyboard, causing the entire body of
screen configurations in front of him to flicker.

*". . . Police are currently seeking an unknown man who
visited the hospital shortly after Ms. Keaghan's death, and
who may unwittingly have further information about the
kidnapping as well as her death . . ."*

Ben? Were they looking for Ben? They knew about him already?' What else had the authorities found out?

Roy looked at the clock on the wall above his partition. Only two p.m. Two more hours to go before he got off work. And he had to pick up that prescription first before he went home.

The letter was in the mail, surely en route to be received tomorrow. It was too soon for things to start going wrong. Too soon!

But what if they did? He looked back at his computer screen and forced himself to take a calming breath. The answer was simple.

If things started to unravel more quickly than he had anticipated or than his plan could stand, he would be prepared. For anything.

Calm again, he started entering codes for another program onto his screen. Only three more days to go. If Alexander forced his hand before then, he *would* be prepared.

Charlie checked his watch by the light of the lamp. Two p.m. When did the man get off work? When would he be home? When would *his* time be up to find that window and possible escape?

He'd been meticulously crawling along the parameters of the basement every minute since he'd awakened from his sleep. For breakfast, the man had fed him oatmeal and juice. He'd felt drowsy almost immediately after having finished the food and drink. Well, starting tomorrow, he had a remedy for that. But now, his time was running out.

He saw a fleck of white dust just a few inches in front of him. He moved a little closer. Was it light?

Charlie passed his hand over the fleck, right where the drywall met the cement foundation of the floor. The fleck disappeared while the whiteness of it hit the back of his little finger.

Charlie sat back on his heels afraid to get excited, afraid not to. Somewhere behind the board in front of him was a source of light.

His window? It had to be. But how could he get to it? He peered hard through the gloom at his watch. Two-twenty-five. He sat back on his heels, still staring at the wall. And saw a tiny crack between the board seams in front of him. How . . . ?

Then he remembered the spoon on his tray beside his bed.

Chapter Nine

They all were gathered in a quiet corner of Jennifer's hotel lounge. Sean sat next to her on a sofa. Clemm and O'Brien were across from them in facing chairs. Jennifer had been expecting some ribbing about the Olin episode from the other two agents, but neither had brought it up. Their dodging the subject was somehow worse.

But that wasn't the issue on the table right here, right now. The story of Judy Keaghan was. And whether she and the missing Ben Keaghan were in on the abduction with others, or flying solo.

"Bob and I will be going back to the Keaghan cabin tomorrow," O'Brien said. "Mauer is prepared to tear it down this time, if he has to."

"Yeah," Clemm said, "there's got to be something inside that was overlooked."

"Judy Keaghan turns out to be his sister, you say?" Sean leaned back.

"According to the insurance form he filled out for Milo's, yeah. She's listed as his beneficiary."

"*And* she's connected to this mysterious Hal, who was most likely the body inside that truck," Jennifer said.

"What's the status on that identification, by the way?" Sean asked O'Brien.

"The fingerprints were nearly burned off. Still, the lab was able to lift a couple, and they're being checked through the headquarters database. So far, no hits."

"Which only means that if the burned guy is Hal, he wasn't ever employed by the government or arrested for another crime," Jennifer pointed out.

"Well, if it's him and he picked this little crime to start with, he picked a spectacular debut," Sean said.

"Anyway, we're still checking," O'Brien concluded.

"All right. What else do we have, Bob? That doctor at the hospital provided a description of this Ben Keaghan. It's out on the national cop wires, right?"

"Yeah. If he doesn't turn up somewhere within the next twenty-four hours, community relations will work with the media, ask Keaghan to come to the police for questioning only."

"Shouldn't take long for him to turn up one way or the other," Jennifer said.

Clemm looked at her. "Clearly."

The other agents looked at Clemm, glanced at Jennifer, then away. Sean said, "I think there's more to be learned from Emily Marsh. She still can probably shed some light on the Judy connection, even if she doesn't yet realize it." He finished the Coke in his glass. "Jennifer and I will check her out again, first thing tomorrow."

Clemm looked at Sean. Sean stared back.

O'Brien cleared his throat. "Well, then, I'll turn in for the night. Bob and I, we'll join Mauer and his people in the morning. Ready, Bob?"

"Sure," the young agent replied. "Night." He stood, encompassing everyone in his general good-bye.

When Jennifer and Sean were alone, she turned the glass of water she held around in her hands. "Thanks."

Sean crossed one leg casually over the other. "For?"

"Sticking up for me. I guess I'm not on Bob Clemm's favorite list right now."

"Bob Clemm is young. He's also good, he'll come around."

Then unexpectedly, Sean chuckled. Jennifer turned her head to look at him. He was looking at her, a smile playing around his lips. "Anybody can make a mistake," he commented mildly. "Even a really big one."

Jennifer searched for words while Sean chuckled again. Then finally, her own lips curved. "Yeah, well, I always say anything worth doing is worth doing right."

"Fuckin' A."

Jennifer laughed outright. Sean's full-bodied response joined hers. When they gradually sobered, each continued to hold the other's eyes.

"Did you realize how much you missed it?" Jennifer asked. At his raised brow, she clarified, "The job."

Sean let the question spin out while he stared into her eyes. The makeup around them was a little smudged now at the end of the day. That imperfection enhanced their unconscious seductiveness. All of her lipstick was gone, too. Her mouth look disturbingly naked. Kissable.

"Well?" Jennifer shifted, feeling a little warm at his look.

"Maybe," he answered finally.

She suddenly was aware that his arm was stretched along the back of the sofa behind her. She imagined she even could feel the warmth of his hand close to the back of her neck. Was he about to touch her? The expression in his eyes said perhaps he wanted to. "What do you mean, maybe?" Her question was soft.

Without moving his arm, Sean leaned toward her a bit.

For a startled moment, Jennifer thought he was going to kiss her. Her breath caught, but she didn't shy away.

Sean's free hand came up to touch the skin at the corner of her mouth. "A piece of hair," he murmured softly, holding his index finger up to show her. Then he leaned away.

Jennifer blinked.

Sean smiled. "To answer your question, if this case hadn't done it, I probably wouldn't have lasted in leisurely solitude for much longer. I'm coming to realize that I wasn't meant for that, no matter how much I thought I wanted it."

"But how do you learn to put it behind you?"

"You don't. You just learn to accept it. Acceptance is one of life's recurring themes in one way or another."

"You're too young to sound," so jaded, she thought, "wise," she finished.

"You're never too young to learn a lesson. About this afternoon, I'm sorry for jumping all over you that hard. I just hate waste, and if anything had happened to you—" He broke off, staring at her.

Jennifer stared back.

"—to any of us, it would have been sheer needless waste."

Jennifer wondered at his passionate declaration. Was he still being philosophical, or personal? If it was the latter, how did she feel about that? A little too touched, maybe. She smiled ruefully at the unpredictability of fate. And if it was personal, wasn't he at all hesitant about their obvious differences?

For one, she'd never seriously considered how she personally felt about an interracial involvement because she'd never been tempted toward one before now. But now, it seemed that an unforeseen and compelling mutual attraction was about to force the question.

So how did she feel about that? A little nervous, yet a little excited too, as any woman contemplating a new man in her life would be.

And as she stared into Sean's watchful brown eyes, she felt something else—the pull of a deep, unnamed emotion. She shook her head, more than a little amazed at her mind's wanderings.

"What have I said now?" Sean asked softly.

"I'm just laughing at myself. Sometimes, I forget to do it." She glanced back up, catching his bemused expression. "It's like the temper, I guess, another fault."

Sean shrugged. "Well, recognition, as they say, is half the battle."

"Again, the sage." Jennifer resisted the urge to lean into him. In fact, though he sat close, she felt much too reluctant to move away. His lashes looked somehow longer this close up. His hair looked darker, too, silky, touchably soft.

And his mouth, she suddenly realized, was no longer smiling. The slight shadow of his beard that bracketed it should have made him look more stern. Instead, its dark contrast against his dusky skin seemed intensely masculine. Exciting.

Jennifer tried to remind herself of why she was here, why they were together. And why that alone demanded she stop feeling so drawn to him.

When Sean's eyes dropped briefly to her lips she made herself lean forward to set down her glass. "I think I'll turn in," she told him softly, starting to rise. Sean stopped her by clasping her hand.

"Wait a minute."

"Why?" Jennifer asked, keeping her back to him, to the expression in his eyes, the edgy tone of his voice.

"Because all of a sudden I feel as if I should apologize for something here."

Jennifer didn't pull away, but she did look down at their joined fingers. "What?" she breathed.

"I'm not sure what," Sean answered, hushed. "You tell me."

What could she possibly say? That she couldn't

remember another man ever tempting her this strongly in her life? That giving into this heated impulse he inspired inside her would be the height of professional folly? "I think," she began, "whatever may be happening between us is moving way too fast."

Sean didn't say anything.

Jennifer gathered the nerve to look at him. He met her stare, held it, then gazed down at their joined hands, too.

"Tell me I'm wrong," she invited.

After a long moment, Sean looked back at her. "You're not wrong." But his concession was slow.

"Sean, it's not—" she tried. "I just don't think it's wise—"

He lifted their hands to his mouth and kissed the back of her cool fingers briefly. Then he let her go. "You don't have to elaborate, Jennifer, I understand." He stood up.

Jennifer felt bereft and almost contradicted herself by asking him to stay. But he beat her to the punch again.

"Neither of us wants added complication to our lives. And no matter what this . . ." he shrugged, "what this attraction is, it could only be that, couldn't it? A complication."

Probably, Jennifer silently conceded. But when he

smiled a little wistfully, she felt uncertain all over again. Then gently, he mocked her caution. "Tell me I'm wrong."

Jennifer only leaned back against the sofa. She hoped he would understand that the most honest answer she could give him right now was her unspoken agreement to let him go.

Sean nodded, still holding her eyes. "Okay, then. I'll see you in the morning. Be ready at nine, I'll pick you up."

"Fine."

Sean walked away. Jennifer watched him all the way through the lobby until he reached the front doors and pushed through. He'd been right to go, she insisted to herself, and she'd been right to let him.

So why did the thought of all of the solitary hours left in the night feel so hollow?

Day Three

Charlie opened his eyes a split second before he heard the key scrape in the lock.

Roy set the tray on the bedside table, as he had done yesterday. He offered Charlie a smile.

Charlie smiled back.

"Good morning."

"Good morning." Charlie guessed the response was expected.

"I made eggs today. I hope you like them scrambled."

Charlie didn't like eggs at all, but he wasn't going to tell the man that. "They look good."

"What do you say, then?"

"Thank you."

Roy nodded. "You're welcome. You're such a good boy." He fell silent, watching Charlie.

Charlie watched him back.

Roy's smile faded slowly. "Well, go ahead, then, eat."

Sighing inwardly, Charlie picked up the fork that had been provided and took off a small bite. The only good thing about this was, it wasn't going to be at all hard to throw them and the medication he guessed they contained back up after the man left. He took a second bite, holding the man's watchful eyes.

Finally, after he'd swallowed the last bit, the man gathered up the tray and asked conversationally, "So, tell me what you're going to do today."

For one startled moment, Charlie stared at him, thinking he'd somehow been discovered. Then he realized he was being silly.

The man was just making strange conversation. In

his head, Charlie answered, *Well, after you get out of here I'm going to go over to that bathroom, stick my finger down my throat, and throw up these nasty eggs. Then, I'm going to take the fork on that tray—if it's a spoon tomorrow, I'll take that—and start picking at that loose board along the wall back there.*

"Cat got your tongue?" Roy pressed.

"No," Charlie said quickly. "I thought after my nap, I'd read a little."

The man nodded, seemingly satisfied with that, and turned away. He had one foot on the stairs when he suddenly stopped and looked back.

Charlie turned his head against the pillow he'd plumped up between the mattress and the wall to look at him. What was wrong with the man today? He seemed jumpy. He really *couldn't* read minds, could he?

"Well, good-bye, then," Roy said. "See you when I get home."

"Bye." Charlie closed his eyes, feigning sleep. Of course, if the man didn't get moving, he wouldn't have to pretend. Whatever he laced the food with worked fast.

Finally, Charlie heard the man's footsteps, then the closing door, then the key in the lock.

He waited a couple of minutes for extra measure, heard the back door to the house slam, then the car outside start and pull out of the drive.

Quickly, Charlie hopped off the bed and hurried to the bathroom. By the time he got there, he already had his finger halfway down his throat.

"Arty, you look like you just swallowed a frog." Special Agent Arty Hopkins's secretary leaned over his shoulder to peer at the letter that had captured his attention. She read the first two sentences then stood up again. Much more soberly, she said, "What exactly do you have there?"

Hopkins looked up, already pulling his phone toward him.

"It's O'Brien, Sean. Bob and I are headed to Lattimore's. You and Jennifer better meet us there."

"What's up?" Sean held the cell phone more closely to his ear as he navigated a tight early-morning-traffic turn. He and Jennifer were less than fifteen minutes away from Emily Marsh's building. But the urgency in O'Brien's tone was unmistakable.

"Hopkins received a letter at headquarters. It would be better for you and Jennifer to see it for yourselves rather than for me to try to explain it over the air."

Sean was already turning the car around. "We're on our way."

*　　*　　*

"What do you mean, we won't give him the money? He's going to kill my little boy two days from now if he doesn't get it!" Paul Lattimore pushed himself away from his study desk and stalked angrily to the picture window overlooking his garden.

Sean knew that while his emotions couldn't be mollified, Paul's intellect *had* to be persuaded if any reasonable rescue effort of Charlie was going to have the chance it needed to work. That also meant they were going to have to level with Paul about Sean's involvement with this, about the very real probability that the entire situation was bigger than his son, Charlie.

Because the letter, which mentioned Jennifer, had left that fact in no doubt:

Okay, it's time for details.
I want the money in all the usual small, untraceable bills these sorts of situations require.

I want them inside a small leather case I want left in a trash can you'll see at the city park at McArther and Lane, at the bench right along the street.

Most importantly, I want the agent the media is calling Alexander's partner, Jennifer, to make the drop. Our boy Sean has already proven that he just can't be trusted with the really big ones—can he?

Thursday, October 8, six p.m., sharp. You won't see me, but I'll see you. And I'll stuff your kid in a box if you fuck me over, Lattimore.

Jennifer walked over to Lattimore and rested her hand on his back. "I know this is hard, but you have to trust us to do our job. Kidnappers get off playing on their victim's emotions. If we actually gave him the money, we'd be giving him critical control of this situation, and we don't want to do that.

"We've had some new leads, some breakthroughs. Most importantly, we still have two days."

"One and a half," Lattimore corrected brittlely.

Jennifer turned her head, looking at Sean, O'Brien, and Clemm. "If our good fortune continues," she told Lattimore, "we won't need until Thursday. And there's every indication such will be the case."

"What indication?"

"Remember what we've told you." They'd explained to him about Ben and Judy Keaghan, and how though Judy was dead, Ben was still involved. They'd assured him it was only a brief matter of time before he was caught by the authorities. After that, they'd know if he was the kidnapper or working with someone else.

Lattimore turned to Jennifer, angrily. "But the upshot is, you don't know that now. You don't know if this Keaghan has my boy, or if it's somebody else who's waiting to cut his throat or whatever before you all even get close." He shook Jennifer's hand off and snapped at Sean. "What do *you* say?"

"I say we all take a breath here, sit down, and discuss possibilities we haven't yet in light of the fact that my role in the Beardsly case in California definitely seems to factor into this now.

"I'm going to ask you again, Paul, can you think of any acquaintances, anyone at all you know of who's expressed an inordinate interest in Charlie? Who's talked about him, inquired about him? Who's made a point to engage you in conversations about children of theirs?"

Paul stared at the floor. He crossed his arms and leaned back against the window sill, deep in thought. Suddenly he raised his head.

Jennifer moved closer to him. "What do you remember?"

This wasn't going to work. Charlie let the fork clatter to the cement floor and sat back on his heels, disheartened.

Almost right off, he'd discovered the fork was too thick to get between the loose boards. And he wasn't strong enough to force the tines in. He'd been trying for nearly an hour. His fingers were so sore, pressing on the metal fork now almost brought tears to his eyes.

He knew that no matter how much the man cared for him and fed him, and tried in his weird way to entertain him, he didn't intend to let Charlie Lattimore out of this house alive. There was just something in his eyes that said when the time came, Charlie Lattimore was going to be dead.

Of course, if he did get out of this alive, his dad would kill him for going off alone, for getting himself kidnapped in the first place. He guessed that thought should have been funny.

But in spite of himself, Charlie did start to cry. Quietly at first, then with low hitching gulps. He couldn't die down here, he *couldn't*!

Desperate, he picked up the fork again, put it against the crack between the boards and leaned on it, trying to use more of his weight. "Work, dammit, *work*!"

He kept muttering through his tears. But it didn't work.

He threw the fork down, watching it skitter to rest at the very base of one of the boards he'd been trying to pry loose. Then he saw a frayed little slit in the very bottom of the board, almost invisible because of the poor light.

Almost, but not entirely.

Leaning closer, his nose almost right up against the wood, Charlie tested the weak part with his finger. A little piece of splinter fell off. Like it was rotten.

Like the wood down there was *rotten*!

He retrieved the fork, put it against this new spot, and inserted the very tip of the tines beneath the jagged place on the wood and the hard wall behind it. Then he pulled up. A bigger chip of wood flaked off, hitting the floor.

Charlie repeated the process. He was rewarded when another piece of wood fell.

"The one who didn't fit," Lattimore explained, looking at Jennifer. "He was the one who wasn't like my other staffers during my election campaign for the state legislature." He shook his head.

"After Cheryl died, I felt lost. I couldn't decide which way to take my career, what to do with my time. So I decided to get back into politics, here on a local level. I poured my energies into organizing the necessary campaign, and a fundamental part of that kind of organization always revolves around volunteers.

"The ones who responded to my campaign were all locals, all born and raised in Indiana or connected to the state somehow. Except for one. His name was, *shit,* I can't—wait a minute. It's written down."

Lattimore walked around his desk and knelt to the double doors of his credenza. From inside, he pulled an oversized ledger and flipped past the first few pages. About halfway through, he motioned to Jennifer.

Sean, O'Brien, and Clemm joined her.

"There," Lattimore said pointing to an entry he'd made last spring. "He's the one, Roy Amory. He's the only one on the team who didn't have any real Indiana ties. Boston, New York, Seattle, and L.A. Those were his former homes, he said. He also told me he didn't have any siblings, that his parents were dead, and that he hadn't made many friends here yet because he'd just moved to town."

"So naturally, you asked him what *had* prompted him to move all the way out here," Sean stated.

"Of course."

"And?"

Lattimore closed the ledger, looking first at Jennifer, then at O'Brien and Clemm, then finally at Sean. "It didn't make sense then. Now it might. God, now it just might."

"What did he *tell* you, Paul?"

"He said he was here to surprise a friend. He said he needed to settle some old business through old family ties."

*　　*　　*

They were back en route to Emily Marsh's office. Jennifer said, "If this Roy Amory moved out here prior to Lattimore's campaign, that would probably put him here about the same time you took your leave from the bureau. After the Beardsly incident, and while your career was in a lull."

"But what's his connection with Paul and me? If Amory is involved in Charlie Lattimore's kidnapping, why would he do it by going through Paul to get to me?"

Jennifer said nothing for long moments. She gazed out at the thick late-morning downtown traffic, thinking. Remembering. *Remembering.*

A late-night conversation between friends. Old friends. A reconciliation of a relationship that had gone tragically off course. A friendship that had been referenced frequently—and publicly—at its height during the years the two men had been earning their individual prominence.

A long-standing friendship about which anyone who kept up with current events would know. She remembered hearing throwaway bits herself, during her own early days with the bureau. The great Sean Alexander, FBI agent extraordinaire, and for a long while after that task force finding, the FBI's agent du jour. Underdog champion and friend to great men.

That last reference was, of course, to Paul Lattimore. Because everyone knew they were close. Like brothers. Like . . .

"Family," Jennifer murmured.

"What?"

She looked over at Sean. "You and Paul Lattimore. For years, it was public knowledge that you two would do anything for each other. That you were as committed to each other as brothers."

Sean's jaw tightened while he watched the road. "Goddamn," he said softly. "Committed. Like family."

From a phone nestled among a deserted bank of them inside Emily Marsh's office building, Sean placed a call.

"Dev, something could be breaking here. I need your help to coordinate a request."

"Of course. Just tell me what, Sean."

Sean proceeded to ask for a California check on two things.

First, what was the status of that Beardsly file he had asked to be faxed? The Indianapolis office hadn't received it yet and they needed it right now. "You've got to get that expedited, Dev."

"And the second request?" Thompson demanded.

Sean wanted to know what they could compile about a one-time Los Angeles resident named Roy

Amory. Specifically, if his name turned up in the Beardsly file and if he carried a criminal record.

"I need anything and everything the field in California is able to come up with, and I need it faxed here."

"You got it. So, this Amory is our boy?"

"It's too early to be sure."

"Your information is on its way."

Chapter Ten

The elevator doors opened, spilling Sean and Jennifer out into the same plush reception area they'd visited only yesterday. They announced themselves to the receptionist, who buzzed Emily Marsh.

"Ms. Marsh is between appointments, right now," the woman informed them. "You're lucky, go right in."

They were already moving by the time the woman stopped talking.

Inside the office, Emily Marsh stayed seated behind her desk, gesturing for Sean and Jennifer to take the couch next to her.

"This is unexpected. How can I help you two today?" She checked her watch. "I'm afraid I only have about twenty or thirty minutes to spare."

Sean said, "Just a few more questions about Judy Keaghan."

"Why?"

"It's fairly clear from the time, place, and method surrounding Charlie's abduction that he was taken by someone who knew his most intimate personal habits."

"My stolen tapes."

"Precisely. Why do you suppose a woman like Judy Keaghan felt motivated to steal them from you?"

"I can't say. I've already told you everything I know."

"Did you ever socialize with your housekeeper?"

"Of course not."

"Did she ever ask to or seem to want to socialize with you?"

"No."

"Did she ever show up at your home on her off days?"

"I don't believe so."

"Are you sure about that or not?"

"Yes, I'm sure."

Jennifer asked, "Did Judy Keaghan ever call you or attempt to contact you in any way that wasn't professional or job-related?"

"I'm sorry I'm sounding like a broken record here, but no."

Sean said, "Have you in the last year, or past few months, or just recently noticed anyone following you?"

Emily suddenly looked arrested. "You mean, like stalking me?"

"Perhaps. Or just seeming to watch your moves. Maybe a stranger in a public place who seemed to stick a little too close to you. Or maybe someone you noticed who kept turning up in the same public places you frequented. Even a stranger who, for some reason, caught your eye?"

Marsh hesitated.

Jennifer pressed, "Have any of those things happened to you?"

"Well, I am remembering something. But it only happened briefly. What I mean is, I'm not sure it meant anything."

"But obviously it was something noticeable enough to cause you concern?"

"Yes, it was then. You see, a few months ago last spring, I thought I was being watched by someone."

"How do you mean, watched?"

"Trailed when I went out. By someone in a car."

"Did you report your suspicions to the police?"

"Well, no, because I wasn't sure I wasn't imagining things. I'd go to the grocery and be waiting for traffic to break on the parking lot so that I could get into the market. And there was this car. I'd be driving out of the garage here and look up in my rearview, thinking I saw the same car behind me.

"Even on the streets sometimes, I'd swear the car

was in an adjacent lane or turning a corner opposite me just as I was turning the other way."

"Sounds pretty unmistakable that something suspicious really was happening," Sean commented. "How come you didn't report it anyway?"

"Because this is real life, Agent Alexander. This is my world, not yours. Things like being followed by some mysterious person just don't happen to people like me."

Sean and Jennifer looked at her.

Emily Marsh sighed. "I just felt funny at the thought of actually doing something as drastic as going to the police when the only thing I could tell them was the make of the car."

"Which was?" Sean asked.

"A blue Buick, I think."

Sean met Jennifer's eyes briefly. A routine Bureau of Motor Vehicles check had revealed Judy Keaghan having a blue 1990 Buick LaSabre registered to her and titled in Indiana.

"We're almost done," Jennifer told her. "Do you recall if any friends of Judy Keaghan ever contacted you? Maybe someone claiming to be a relative, or a friend who called your home looking for her?"

"No, I'm sure not."

"Do you know anyone, or have any patients named Roy Amory?"

"No, I don't."

"Do you know if Judy knew anyone by that name?"

"Wait a minute, *Roy!*"

"You *do* know a Roy Amory?" Sean asked.

"Not me, Judy. I mean she never mentioned any last names, but I do recall commenting to her one day not long before she quit that she was looking particularly chipper. She laughed and told me it must have been because her boyfriend, Roy, was back in town."

"Do you know anything else about him?" Jennifer asked.

"Only what I thought was so odd at the time. Judy told me she'd met him at my house one day while I was at work. He showed up on the doorstep, the proverbial traveling salesman, trying to sell her a vacuum cleaner."

"And he made the sale?"

"Not of the cleaner, but of something else. She said she'd been smitten right away, and from the way she talked I guess he returned her interest. At any rate, she told me he asked her out on the spot."

"She didn't share any more personal details with you about this Roy?"

"Well, to be honest, I wasn't that interested." Marsh hesitated. "But looking at both your faces now, I guess I should have encouraged the conversation."

Sean stood up. Jennifer did, too. Sean thanked Emily Marsh again for her time.

In the car, Jennifer said, "So I'm thinking if this Roy Amory pans out in California, we could be looking at a scenario that could go something like this. Amory gets close to Paul Lattimore by volunteering to work on his campaign.

"He becomes a casual friend and in the course of their relationship learns from Lattimore about Charlie and Emily Marsh. Operating on the principal that the way to get to you is to go through Lattimore's boy, he figures he has to find a way to get close to Charlie."

Sean picked it up. "At some point, kidnapping comes to his mind. Through casual conversation with Paul, he figures out how to do some checking on Emily Marsh. He finds out she employees a cleaning service and when. He persuades Judy Keaghan, whom he's met at some point after his arrival late last winter, to get a job with Marsh's cleaning service so that she can maneuver herself into Marsh's home as his plant."

"But how would the others come in?" Jennifer demanded. "Say she goes along with a wild scheme of his because she thinks she's in love. What would motivate her brother and this man, Hal?"

"That's easy, Agent Bennett. That other great motivator besides love. Money."

O'Brien, Clemm, and Mauer stood in the middle of Ben Keaghan's cabin. The living room's furnishings were as sparse as they'd been the first time through and still didn't reveal anything. The back bedroom, as well as the bedroom next to it held meager assortments of jeans and shirts. They could all have belonged to a man, or they could have been unisex grunge.

"We've searched every stick and board in this place," Mauer observed in disgust.

It suddenly occurred to Clemm, "What about *under* the boards?"

The three looked at each other. Mauer walked around the agents to the front door. "Dave!" He called one of his deputies. "Get the boys back in here."

Twenty minutes later, Clemm found the stash under the bed in the back bedroom, under a floor board that looked to have been pried loose then readhered with some sealant they would analyze later. Wrapped inside a woman's black dress, blue trench coat, and tucked inside a blue ball cap were Emily Marsh's tapes. Next to the tapes was Judy Keaghan's diary. It was marked for 1998 through 1999.

The final entry was dated October third. The day before Charlie Lattimore's kidnapping.

Clemm took the diary into the living room where there was better midafternoon light to see by.

At the dining room table, he, Mauer, and O'Brien studied the entries.

October 2, 1999
Dear Diary,
Almost time. Everything's set. Roy left ten minutes ago, and Hal and Ben have both gone to sleep. I hope we don't have to kill the boy. But if we do, we will.

October 1, 1999
Dear Diary,
I spent last night at Roy's. He says we shouldn't be together again until all of this is over. None of us should be seen hanging around together, he says, because someone might remember it later and report it to the police. I'm sure going to miss him. I'll be glad when it's done and he and the boy are at the house. It's a nice house, too nice, I teased him, for something like this. But the country is always fine.

Clemm skimmed the next few entries, because they were mostly exposition about Judy's feelings for Roy. However, he quickly found an insert of more interest.

Pressed between two blank pages was a wallet-sized photo.

It was of a thin-faced, dark-haired woman, late twenties or so. Even though she had lines of hard living already etched into her face, she was a modestly pretty woman.

Clemm turned the photo over. Penciled in on the back was 1991. Philly. —J.

Clemm remembered the charred victim who had fought for life in a nearby hospital. He flipped a few pages back. And found the second small revelation of the day.

Inside a single envelope was a photocopied sheet of paper and another photo. This photo was a Polaroid. In it were three subjects: Judy and two men. One was dark-haired, the other fair and seemingly younger than his companions.

Clemm turned the photo over. Printed in pencil on the back were three names: Judy, Ben, Hal. Philly.

"What's the paper?" Mauer asked.

Clemm unfolded it, skimmed down its contents for a few seconds, then passed it around. When it reached Mauer, the older man said, "Well, I'll be damned."

The page was a photocopy of a certificate of adoption. It was dated 1972, and the adopted child listed was Hal Keaghan.

Back at Indianapolis headquarters, Jennifer's ear was pressed to one phone while Sean commandeered another.

Jennifer was listening to Mauer. "Adopted? All right, stay in touch. And Sheriff, let's get an all-points bulletin out for that Buick plate." After a moment she asked, "How are we doing with Ben Keaghan?" Then, "Okay, we'll handle it."

She disconnected and punched in an internal extension connecting her to community relations.

Across from her, Sean was saying, "Yeah, Dev, it's—wait a minute, somebody's talking to me." He put his hand over the mouthpiece and swiveled in his chair. "Yeah, Hopkins, what is it?"

"Stuff's coming over on the fax, addressed to you."

Sean took his hand away. "It's coming over now. What about the other?" He listened a moment. "You're kidding. Not even a speeding ticket? Or jaywalking?" He listened some more. "What kind of organization is that? Yeah, well, tell me as soon as you know."

Hopkins laid a thick stack of paper on the blotter in front of Sean, who said, "Gotta go. Okay, thanks, man." His disconnected receiver hovered over the console. "Hopkins, any prints on Amory's letter?"

"Yes. Still being checked."

"This is it? The Beardsly file?" Jennifer took the chair beside Sean's desk just as he finished hanging up.

"This is it. Let's split it."

Jennifer was already scooping a handful of pages off the top.

The file in its entirety consisted of what Sean had suggested it would. There were photos of the school, taken from different angles and perspectives. Building plans were present, too.

There were lists of the students who had been in the building the day Albert Brady and his men had taken siege. There was a list of weekend personnel, the teacher who had died, and another general list of school officials.

And there were the names of parents and guardians for the children who had died.

Jennifer and Sean had been reading through their respective stacks for no more than ten minutes when Sean's eye fell on a name. "Look at this," he said.

Charlie was just putting the board back into place when he heard the car in the driveway. It was four-thirty. He should have stopped at least an hour ago in order to get things completely tidy instead of just shoving the splinters that had fallen on the floor into a dark corner.

After that first little bit of board gave, the rest started coming easier. He could insert the tines now, from the bottom to about halfway up.

At one point, he'd pulled a little on the bottom of the board. Sure enough, behind it at the top was a small rectangular window. It worried him for a moment, until he remembered he was small too. And determined. And he had the whole day tomorrow after the man went away.

Now, he had to prop the board back in place and make sure he didn't have any wood dust on his clothes, in his hair, or on his face. He started when the back door slammed.

Quickly, he darted into the makeshift little bathroom. With both hands, he did a quick brush off of his clothes, hair, and face, although he didn't think there was too much to brush off. And if there was, the man never went into his bathroom anyway. Whatever wood hit the floor probably would stay undetected until he could clean it up tomorrow.

The key scraped in the lock just as Charlie dived for the bed and the book he'd pretend to be reading.

Roy started down the stairs. He was breaking habit today. On the tray were two chicken salad sandwiches, one for him as well as the boy. His eyes automatically checked the accompanying chips, napkins, canned sodas, and plates. His inner thoughts were still preoccupied with what he'd heard only less than an hour ago, coming over the radio.

The police wanted Ben to come in for questioning only? Fat chance. They knew something and were waiting to nail Ben's butt. Which, of course, Ben knew. Which meant they were seriously hunting Ben and that it was only a matter of time before they caught him.

Which meant it was only a matter of time before they knew about him, too.

On the other hand, everything would be over in two days anyway, so perhaps Ben didn't matter. Perhaps he should stop worrying about Ben and concentrate on spending an evening of quality time with his boy.

Charlie laid the book down when the man said, "Hi. How was your day?"

"Okay. How was yours?"

Roy smiled. He liked that concern. "Hectic, long. But now I'm home. I fixed us chicken salad tonight. It's one of my best dishes. If you want, when you finish that sandwich, you can have more."

Charlie picked up his food and took a bite. The man sounded depressed tonight. Sad. He sat down on a corner of the bed and Charlie scooted his legs over, so that there would be plenty of room without the man having to even accidentally touch him.

Roy was halfway through his sandwich when he said, "Do you ever think about heaven, boy?"

Charlie's eyes shot to his. The cola in his mouth almost went down the wrong way.

"Hm?" Roy asked.

"Well, I guess. Doesn't everybody?"

"No, I don't mean sort of. I mean specifically. Ever

203

think about what it would be like, about what God would say? What He'd look like?"

"I think He'd look nice." He did *not* want to have this conversation. "You never did tell me what you do at work."

Roy looked at him, wondered why his hair looked so light when this morning it had been dark. He always thought it odd, his hair being dark when his own was so light and his mother's was just a little bit browner than that.

"Sir? Are you all right?" Charlie set his unfinished sandwich down. He had a funny feeling and couldn't force down any more.

Roy just stared at him a little longer. Then he smiled. He reached out and brushed a stray piece of that strange light hair away from Charlie's eyes. That was another thing. He always kept his bangs short, how had they grown so long so quickly?

Charlie swallowed. He couldn't move. As the man had reached out to brush at his forehead, Charlie's eyes had dropped down to the portion of trouser belt concealed beneath the man's jacket. A gun was tucked there.

"Here it is." Sean laid the paper he was looking at on the desk between them, turning it so that Jennifer could clearly read the names.

Two names down the page, Jennifer saw it. "Roy

Amory was the *vice principal*? You've got to be kidding."

"Ben, you should go in, you know. That little boy's survival could depend on you."

Ben Keaghan zipped his pants while he dispassionately watched the naked blonde on the bed. She didn't even have the modesty to cover herself up. Just kept lying there, splayed open, as if he were still inside her. She disgusted him.

"How much do I owe you?" Now that she'd eased his tension by servicing him, he just wanted to get out of this motel and back to the anonymity of the streets.

The woman's coy smile slipped a little. "Well, if you were to agree to stay a while, I was considering chalking this one up as a freebie." She raised her hands to her breasts and squeezed them, making her large nipples stand out. "Whaddaya say, baby? You make me hot again just watching you."

If he had his knife on him, he'd cut her lying mouth. As it was, he simply repeated, "I said, how much."

The woman's smile suddenly fell completely away. She closed her legs and finally pulled the threadbare colorless spread over herself. "Your dick ain't gold, honey. Fifty. Same as I'd charge anybody else."

Ben buttoned his shirt, tucked it in, and pulled his

wallet from his back pocket. He counted out the bills and threw them at her. He just missed hitting her in the face.

"Bastard!" she hissed at the closing door. She picked up the money and recounted, feeling sorry for herself in spite of it. Then she looked at the phone.

She couldn't remember. Had that news reporter said anything about a reward?

"Sarah, I said turn that television off now, tonight's a school night."

"But Mommy, it's that man."

Carol Loring was barely listening. She had the baby to bathe, the dishes to wash, and seven-year-old Sarah, who was in another one of her cantankerous moods, to tuck in before she herself could go to bed.

"Mommy?"

"What?"

"Come look, it's that man!"

Carol reluctantly set the cold casserole dish on the table and turned back around. She hated when Jack was out of town on business trips. Inevitably, things got their craziest around here when he was gone and unavailable to help out.

"Okay, Sarah, here I am. What are you going on about?"

Sarah pointed at the television. "Look."

Carol looked. "Oh my God," she said, sounding mildly amazed.

". . . *Authorities have now identified him as Hal Keaghan, a twenty-seven-year-old welder whose last-known residence was in Morgan County. Keaghan's burned corpse was discovered in the furniture truck found burned four days ago in a stretch of Southern Indiana woods, near the estate from where Charlie Lattimore was abducted. Paul Lattimore . . ."*

"See Mommy, I told you. It's that man who was peeing on the road."

Carol frowned. She was wondering if first thing in the morning, school should be delayed in favor of a visit to the police. If this Hal Keaghan was dead, what had happened to that other man? The one she and Sarah could both visually identify?

That poor little boy, Charlie Lattimore. "Come on, Sarah, that's it. Bedtime." Carol reached over to turn off the set. She ignored her daughter's reflexive whining and took her hand.

If they left first thing, she could have Sarah in class by no later than nine a.m., which would mean she wouldn't have to miss so much school. On the other hand, she could pull her out of school a little early, which would be more convenient for her day and save *her* time. Still, getting involved in something like this . . .

"Good night, Mommy." Sarah planted a wet kiss

on her mother's lips as Carol bent over to tuck her in. "I love you, Mommy," she said before she turned over to go to sleep.

Such a little angel, Carol thought. And Charlie Lattimore was only ten. His poor father. What must he be going through. She turned out Sarah's light and backed out of the room.

A police drawing of that other man, maybe. She and Sarah could help with that. What if it were Sarah who had been abducted from her? Offering some kind of visual to help them find the other kidnapper was the least they could do.

Chapter Eleven

Day Four

*The sky was too blue, the air too clear, the day too glisten-
ing and crisp for anyone to die. And yet they would.
Because they must.*

*Roy sat on the grassy rise all alone, wishing he could
be inside the school with his son. Wishing he hadn't had
to call in this morning with a feigned illness so that he
could be here instead of carrying out His plan.*

*Sam would be frightened. His little boy wouldn't know
how to handle his fear, how to find the courage to be
strong. Because all his life, Sam's mother and father had
been strong for him.*

*And then, since last summer just his father after a
drunken motorist had taken his sweet, gentle mother out
of his life forever. Roy felt a tear slip down his face,
then another.*

He thought of how Sam wouldn't understand why his

father had to be strong for not only him, but all the little children who were God's chosen messengers on Earth.

Roy held the binoculars up to study Albert. The others were inside, and they were inconsequential. They would do as they were told. They always did.

It was up to Albert now. Albert and Roy.

And Sean Alexander, the FBI man who, the radio update periodically revealed, was now negotiating with Albert. The other hostage negotiator who had been talking for hours had quit. For the Irishman.

Sean Alexander held Sam's life in his hands. And Albert's. And the children's. Sean Alexander didn't know it, but he, too, was destined this day to be an instrument of fate.

Roy raised the binoculars again. And caught his breath. What was Albert doing? Roy reached over, keeping the binoculars where they were while he notched the radio up. He also picked up his walkie-talkie and activated it.

A terse, "Yes?" answered on the other end.

"What's happening outside? I can't tell by looking from here."

"Alexander's making a move, he—"

"I need to hear. There's a television in the corner by the chalkboard. Turn it on, then put your radio up to it so that I can get this live, straight into my ear." Roy waited tensely for less than a minute, then heard, ". . . Alexander appears to be getting through. Lisa, can you see from your vantage point down there?"

"Yes, Carl, you're right. Albert Brady is saying something to Alexander, and Alexander is answering back. He's, wait a minute, okay yes. He's putting on more protective gear and signaling to the rest of his men to do the same."

"Can you tell, Lisa, is he going in? Is it going to be a forcible run on Brady and his gang?"

"Hold on, Carl, something's happening. Alexander's holding up his hand to the agents behind them. He appears to be signaling them to stand by. I'm sorry, Carl, it's all very tense and very confusing down here . . ."

"That's all right Lisa. To our listening audience, you're hearing a live broadcast on KKLB-TV. We're going to stay with this hostage situation as it develops. Lisa what's happening now? . . ."

Roy understood. He didn't need any damn newsreader now to clarify. Albert was giving up. "No!" Roy whispered, bringing his binoculars back up with one hand. Albert appeared to be listening to Alexander, hanging on every word, in fact. Jeopardizing their cause and the immortal souls of those poor children they were going to send to God.

So that the people of the nation would know what happened, what must happen to pure little souls who were being systematically corrupted. "Albert," he whispered, "don't!"

". . . Lisa, it appears as if Brady's about to surrender, is that right?"

"I think it is, Carl. Alexander is doing a masterful job talking him down. I've never seen such calm, such control. Brady appears to actually be preparing to lay his detonator down on the ground. Those children are going to get out after all. They . . . oh, Carl, oh wait! Oh no, God no . . . !"

Roy heard, *". . . lay his detonator down. Those children are going to get out after all . . ."* Albert, don't! Roy thought frantically. He picked up his own detonator, twin to the one Albert and the others believed was the only one their collective money had purchased. But Roy had suspected even then that Albert was weak. Roy had known to be prepared. *Albert, please,* he begged now silently.

". . . Oh, Carl . . ."

Roy let the binoculars drop and dangle from their cord around his neck. He didn't need to see anymore, couldn't look. *Sean Alexander, this is your fault! I hate you, hate you—I'll kill you, too!*

Roy pushed the button.

". . . Oh, wait! Oh, no, God no! . . ."

Roy dropped the detonator to the grass. He dropped his head to his hands and sobbed. *Sam, Sam, I love you!*

Roy tossed and turned, still muttering the words in his sleep. *Sam, I love you. Sam . . . !* With a gasp, he reared up in his bed, leaving the nightmare behind. His pajamas were drenched with sweat. His heart was thundering. In his mind's eye it was still all so fresh. His boy was dying. Again. And again. And again.

As he had in the dream, he dropped his head in his hands and sobbed like a baby. Because he'd killed his baby, his *baby*.

Sean Alexander had killed his baby!

"Should we go in do you think?" Bob Clemm waited for O'Brien's answer while they both surveyed the engineering firm and flood of lunchtime employees who poured inside. "No, we'll risk too many strange looks, and if he intercepts any one of them he may run. We'll park out here and watch for him before he gets inside."

"There's a space over there, then." Clemm pointed to the front row of cars directly across from the entrance to the sprawling one-story building.

O'Brien passed another car to reach it, then backed in. They had a clear look at anyone coming or going inside the building's door.

When Roy Amory arrived, they would take him.

One fifty-five p.m.

Roy pulled into the company parking lot. He was running ten minutes late and irritated about it. He was never late. But he'd had trouble focusing all morning in the wake of the dream.

And then Charlie had barely said two words to him before he'd left this morning. Instead, he'd just mumbled and nodded and stared at him all wide-eyed.

Roy was not in a good mood. All he wanted to do now was punch the clock before two, and there probably weren't any damn spaces left because everybody else was rushing back from lunch, too. And he wanted to be left totally alone with his work and thoughts once he was inside.

He was circling around the back when he thought he saw a space one row from the front. That's when his eye just happened to skip forward enough to catch sight of the dark sedan that was parked in the front row with two men sitting inside.

Roy's foot backed off the accelerator instinctively. Who were they? Surely not employees. Even the last of the stragglers rushed to clock in by two. And these two were making no move to get inside.

Roy hit the brake, sitting in the side aisle adjacent to the row and its empty space he'd spotted. The answer was obvious. They weren't moving because they didn't belong inside. Were they cops? Had they come for him? Had they already taken Ben and had Ben told them about him?

Roy carefully put the car in reverse. They still

weren't moving, which meant they hadn't noticed his car sitting to the side. If he backed up slowly, he could get away unseen.

The cops were going to force his hand, make him do what he didn't want to do too soon. Somebody was going to die.

Roy watched for oncoming traffic, waited impatiently for one slow-moving car to pass and checked his rearview while that car crawled by. The car with the two suited men in it still hadn't moved.

But he did. Out onto the busy street in back of the building. Heading back to where he'd come from. To Charlie. He wanted to see Charlie.

He didn't even realize as he drove slowly down the street that he started to cry.

"Yes, Paula?" Hopkins set his coffee down on his desk and settled in as he listened to the office receptionist's page.

"There's a woman and a little girl here to see either Sean or Jennifer. I told her neither of them were in, and that maybe they could see you."

"*Who* is it?"

"They say they saw Hal Keaghan with another man in the vicinity of the kidnapping the morning it happened. They want to know if they can help."

Hopkins was out of his chair almost before the

receptionist finished explaining. "I'm on my way up," he told her, and hung up his phone.

The board came away from the wall so suddenly, Charlie fell backward with the momentum. He'd been working all morning, and now beautiful afternoon light spilled down from the window. The grime on the glass dimmed the illumination, but it was daylight, nonetheless. Charlie was dazzled by the sun. But not for too long.

He had to figure a way to get out of that window. And though he had time, he didn't have all day to do it. And he had to do it.

Before last night, the man had never carried a gun downstairs with him. And though the man had sat by his side for a long time after they'd finished dinner, he'd seemed distracted. He'd looked at Charlie as if he didn't see him, though he touched him constantly—to stroke his hair, to squeeze his arm, to pat his leg.

Charlie looked around the room for something that would help him. On the far wall close to his bed, he spotted a thin wooden chair. On his way to get it, he thought about how he'd hated hearing the man coming down the stairs each morning, then again at night to feed him. He'd hated pretending that he hadn't minded having a conversation with him when all the man really did was give him the creeps.

But he knew, as he dragged the chair across the room, that if he spent another few hours with the man like the ones they'd shared last night, he wasn't going to be able to hide his fear. And somehow, he thought the fact that he *did* manage to hide it was maybe the only thing keeping him alive.

Because it was the only thing keeping the man calm.

Charlie stood back from the chair, dusting his hands against his pants. The cane bottom looked frayed at the edges, as if the seat were already falling out. Charlie lifted his face to the window then extended his arm against the wall to get some sense of how tall he was going to have to be to get out.

He looked back at the chair. If he fell through, he could hurt himself pretty badly, but somehow he thought a bad scrape would be the least of his worries if the man came downstairs and found him out. Testing the seat, he put a fist against it and pushed down with all his weight.

It held. And it also was his only real hope to get up to the window and out. Still . . . he put both fists against it and pressed again. The seat continued to hold. Well . . . Charlie put one foot on the chair and both hands against the wall, so that the concrete would take at least part of his weight.

So far so good. He brought the other leg up. And heard a tiny crack. Quickly, he leaned against the wall again and raised his head. The window wasn't more than half an inch above him. Taking a deep breath, he brought his hands away from the wall . . . and heard another small rip. But he stood as he was.

And was rewarded when the chair held.

Roy briefly took one hand off the steering wheel to wipe the moisture from his eyes. He glanced at his wristwatch, then put his hand back on the wheel.

How could it be four o'clock? He looked at the gas gauge. It was almost on empty. A frightened little jolt tugged at him as he drove through the intersection and pulled into a station to get some gas.

How could he have been so *unaware* that he was losing two hour's worth of time? Had he been driving all this time? Or had he stopped somewhere? At a diner for coffee? For something to eat?

He had to get hold of himself. Charlie would panic if he saw him this way, and he didn't want the boy to panic. He wanted Charlie to like him. Trust him. Maybe even love him.

As he loved Charlie. He was so good. So brave and sweet. The perfect little boy, the perfect little son. Lattimore couldn't appreciate how perfect and didn't deserve to have him anymore. But Roy didn't care about Lattimore.

He cared about Sean, about making him see Charlie for what he was. A chosen angel. A messenger of God.

I'm coming, Charlie, he thought as he drove, feeling comforted by his thoughts. *I'm coming, my son.*

Charlie couldn't believe it. The glass in the window was cracked. When he pushed on it just a little at first to test it, a portion of it actually gave. He saw it fall away, heard it hit the grass outside.

The problem was, how was he going to get all of it out without cutting his hands or the rest of himself if he managed to crawl out? He looked back over his shoulder. The bedspread?

It was thin enough for him to manage, but big enough to create some bulk around his fisted hands. He looked down at his sneakered feet and thought, But what about this chair.

It was holding him now, but he didn't trust it would hold him again if he climbed down, then strained it even further by trying to climb back up.

Which meant he was trapped here? Dammit, *no.* It couldn't mean that.

His shirt. A spurt of hope caused him to take a short little excited breath. He wouldn't have to move from where he was to get his hands wrapped inside his shirt.

Moving carefully so that he wouldn't abruptly shift his weight against the fragile chair, Charlie curled his hands in the hem of his shirt and, slowly, started to pull it over his head.

Could he wait until tomorrow, or would his faith compel him to do it tonight? Roy thought of the gun, loaded now, in the nightstand beside his bed. He thought of the note that had suggested to Jennifer and Lattimore, and most importantly, Sean, that nothing was going to happen until a transaction took place inside a deserted park in broad daylight.

But that had been before Ben had become the target of a manhunt. Which meant the same hunters would ultimately find *him.* And the hunt for Ben had been launched before those two at his firm had been dispatched to watch for him.

Could he wait until tomorrow? Or would his faith compel him to do it tonight? He was still debating as he turned a corner, a fourth of a mile from the house.

Charlie closed his eyes, turned his head, and punched at the glass with his cloth-protected hands. The chair scooted backward a little, and he caught his breath. The glass hadn't broken, but he'd felt it wobble.

He drew his hands back, then brought them forward, hard. The chair didn't move this time, but the glass did. A big chunk of it broke jaggedly away from the rest and fell outside onto the grass.

Charlie could hear the faint distant barking of a dog, smell the clean fresh odor of newly mown grass wafting faintly, then less faintly on the undulating autumn air. His pulse started to pound. He was going to make it, he really was! He drew back his hands again.

Roy turned onto the street two blocks from his house. He'd given up listening for his answer. He'd turned the dilemma over to God.

In his mind's eye, he saw the gun and thought, let *Him* decide.

The last of the glass fell out. Charlie was breathing hard now, from exertion, from excitement, from fear. Where would he go after he was outside the house? He hadn't seen any others close by the night the man had brought him here.

On the other hand, all of that land directly across from the house did have fence around it, which meant it had to belong to somebody. Which meant that, no matter how far he had to walk, somebody there or nearby there might be at home.

But first things first, he warned himself. First, he had to get out of this house.

Making sure that his hands were still wrapped inside his shirt, Charlie managed to curl his fingers around the sill as best he could. Then he placed one foot, then the other, against the cement wall, like a mountain climber putting one foot in front of the other. In that manner, he slowly but effectively climbed up the basement wall.

And heard what sounded like a car drive by on the road. Was it somebody who could have helped, if he'd already been out there to flag them down? Gritting his teeth in determination, Charlie tried to get a better grip on the sill. Then he started pulling himself up again.

In the distance, he heard another sound. Another car? Another chance? His face was even with the open air coming through the broken window now. And a car was coming closer, he could hear it! Grunting with effort, Charlie managed to get his head through the opening, to squeeze his shoulders through, then his chest.

The T-shirt he wore protected his skin only a little from the jagged edges of glass still sticking up around the sill. But he wouldn't let himself pay attention to the minor cuts he felt when glass poked through fabric to his skin.

The car was too close, coming down the street from the other side of the house!

Roy turned off the easy-listening radio station he'd had tuned in as he pulled into the driveway. Digging into his pants pocket for his keys, he was walking around the front of the car with his head down when he thought he heard something from the other side of the house.

Charlie was so startled he almost scrambled back reflexively through the tight hole he'd just climbed out of.

It was *him*. Charlie stood frozen in the pile of glass outside the broken window. His shirt was clutched in his hands, little spots of blood dotted the torso and back of his undershirt. He imagined he could hear footsteps in the grass around the corner and knew in that instant he couldn't go back.

He turned toward the field across the yard, toward all those tall dead stalks of corn that filled it. And he ran.

What the *hell*! Roy rounded the house at a dash, half-expecting to see nothing. He couldn't believe his eyes were seeing what he'd only thought he'd heard.

Before he had time to consciously think about it or feel the full anger and panic that drenched him, Roy was running, too.

"*Charlie*! Charlie, you'd better get back here right now, boy! You're gonna be *sorry*."

Charlie gasped as the furious shout reached him. He stumbled a little but kept running while he threw a look over his shoulder. He gasped and faced forward again, not looking back after that. Because he didn't want to see that awful expression on the man's face again.

The man had promised it once, inside the confines of a small, musty, deserted car. His expression said it all over again.

The man was going to kill him.

"*Charlie!* You little bastard, come *back* here!" And then the man started to laugh because he was gaining. He was still laughing as Charlie suddenly went down hard on one knee, wobbled a little when he got up, and took off again.

Roy's feet pounded the dirt as relentlessly as the waves of icy anger rushing through him battered his mind. God was deciding. Even as he chased the boy, even as the boy continued to run, God was embracing Roy in His golden judgment light.

Charlie started to cry. He could hear the man right behind him now. *Daddy, I don't want to die. Please, God, don't let me die!*

Roy didn't even hear himself roar in triumph and fury when his extended hands connected with the boy and grabbed him.

"No! No!" Charlie sobbed.

"Shut up!" Roy jerked the boy so violently his head snapped back then forward again. Charlie seemed more than a little dazed as he lost his footing and stumbled against Roy.

"Don't hurt me, mister! Please just let me go."

"Stop begging!" Roy shook him again. The boy just continued to cry. The red haze in front of Roy's eyes thickened. He raised a hand above the boy's face, determined to cower him down.

Charlie continued to sob and braced for the blow. What did it matter, he thought? *I'm already dead . . .*

Then they both heard the car.

Roy's hand fell and his head snapped up. He looked wildly around.

Charlie felt a sudden burst of strength too, and of hope. If he could only yell, scream, draw attention—

Roy clamped his hand over Charlie's mouth.

Charlie grunted and twisted as violently as he could within the man's grip. And then he saw a car coming up over the hill of the road in the distant horizon. He struggled harder.

The man suddenly wrapped his free arm around Charlie's chest like a wrestler taking an opponent in a bone-crushing hold. Abruptly, Charlie went limp, his cries tapering off to a wounded, pitiful moan. Seizing the advantage the man turned him until his own body shielded most of the boy from the road and from the unwanted motorist's sight.

The pain was too much! Charlie couldn't breathe. Everything was dimming. Was he passing out? No, please, not after all the effort, all the struggle, all the pain. He couldn't be passing out. He couldn't be letting this man *win*.

Roy held the limp boy in a vicelike grip against his side. To the casual eye, he knew it would appear as if a man and a boy—perhaps his son—were just standing companionably together, just communing with nature.

Roy even waved to the motorist behind the wheel, who actually smiled and waved back as he passed, drew farther away, then finally disappeared over another hill in the road.

Roy looked down at his unconscious charge. To his utter surprise, he felt numb. The fury that had ridden him so hard just breathless minutes ago was all gone, already a dissipated memory. Was that emotion awaiting him back at the house?

Like the gun? Like the aftermath of the decision God had shown him in a burst of light?

Slowly, Roy turned back toward the house, bringing Charlie around with him. Because it was easier, he bent his knees to get better purchase and picked Charlie up, cradling him like a baby within his arms.

Could he wait until tomorrow? Or would his faith compel him to do it tonight?

Sean realized Hopkins was waiting for him as soon as he walked inside the office and the man looked up.

"What?" Sean bypassed his own desk to get the reason for the excitement he saw in the younger man's eyes.

"Two ladies are here you ought to talk to." He looked beyond Sean. "I thought Jennifer would be back from lunch by now, where is she?"

"She's right here," Jennifer answered coming through the door juggling her purse in one hand and a mug of coffee from the community pot the receptionist had refreshed. "What have we got?"

Hopkins waited until she'd walked over to join him and Sean. "These two ladies here," he turned to smile at the cute little girl, who smiled back, "they saw footage of Hal Keaghan on the news last night. Sarah says she saw him peeing on the side of a road the day Charlie Lattimore was kidnapped."

Jennifer's eyes shifted to the mother then the child.

"Even better," Hopkins was still saying, "she also saw him standing there with his pal." Hopkins turned a little to call a man who sat quietly observing from two desks down. "Jack, bring it over here."

Jennifer and Sean watched the other agent approach.

Hopkins urged, "Show them," then stepped around to his own desk where he picked up a manilla file.

The other agent said, "Little girl's got good eyes. She says she could only see part of their faces. But her description was clear as a bell." He held out a sketch, face up, that he'd drawn not thirty minutes ago. In it, a man with thinning light hair, light eyes, and who was clean-shaven, stood glaring out of the image into the quiet breathless air.

"Now look at this," Hopkins said, holding up a personnel photo from the Beardsly file. Except for the beard on the subject in the photo, the two men— the one on paper and the one in Jack's hands—presented an exact match.

Sean looked up at Hopkins. Then he turned to Jennifer, who nodded slightly and sighed.

They had their two phony delivery men. One was Hal Keaghan. The other, thanks to a concerned mother's support of her observant little child, had just been corroborated. He was Roy Amory.

"There's more," Hopkins commented, causing Sean and Jennifer to turn to him. "Some more goodies came in on the fax. Seems there may be more to Roy Amory than anyone could have suspected even now." He set the file of faxes he held down on a desk. "So, do we go get him?"

"No one's heard from O'Brien and Clemm yet?" Sean answered.

Hopkins conceded with an impatient shrug.

"Call Mauer and tell him to issue the police alert. While you're doing that, Jennifer and I are going to go through these faxes. With continued luck, this information might take us exactly to wherever Roy Amory is hiding."

When Charlie came to, his hands were tied tightly to his sides. His feet were trussed together, too. He turned his head and his heart jumped.

The man was leaning against the wall beside the bed. His arms were folded across his chest.

In one of his hands, he held the gun. His eyes maintained a fixed stare Charlie knew was a threat. "He has spoken while you slept," Charlie heard him say. Then the man pushed away from the wall and turned halfway toward the steps.

"Good night, son," Roy told Charlie. "I love you."

Charlie watched the man's back until the shadows swallowed him.

Chapter Twelve

"Let's see what we've got." Sean spread the faxed papers so that they were within everyone's reach. He, Jennifer, Clemm, and O'Brien were grouped around a small table in a meeting room Jennifer's hotel management had given them off the lobby.

A little more than an hour earlier the four of them had shared dinner in one of the hotel's restaurants. O'Brien and Clemm had been called in from the field. Sean and Jennifer had agreed with them that since they all needed to eat while they still had some uninterrupted time to do it, they should gather someplace where they could do business afterward without having to backtrack to the office.

At random, each agent picked up some of the papers that detailed Roy Amory's recent past. They also compared them to the documents inside the Beardsly file, which Sean had brought along. They studied a mixture of documents that detailed the founding of the Beardsly school twenty years before, as well as collections of news stories and academic noteworthiness it had achieved throughout the years.

Interspersed with the school information was that about its employees, some of whom were teachers recognized for other services they'd performed for the developmentally challenged within the community. Jennifer held Amory's photo.

Roy Amory didn't look like a killer. Even though to the best of their knowledge Charlie still lived, three other men and a woman who probably were his accomplices had died. Amory's smile was too gentle, his eyes too soft. The arm he had around the boy hugged to his side in the photo was too protective.

Jennifer sighed. She felt compelled to look up in that moment and caught Sean's eye.

"Got something?" he asked.

O'Brien and Clemm gazed up, waiting for her answer. "It's just the irony. So often the ones who look the gentlest are the ones who seem to harbor the wildest delusions. According to all of this, Amory was respected by his faculty and community and well-liked by the children he administered."

"Which goes to show you really never know," Clemm said.

O'Brien tossed a set of papers on top of the general

pile. "Look at these, our terrorists also seem to have led some interesting lives."

Each of the others picked up pages from those papers, read, and passed documents along the conference table to the next colleague in line. Minutes later, O'Brien said, "For a trio of boys who hadn't done anything much in their lives except talk big, they sure went out in style."

"Except, why would they suddenly want to go out?"

Sean, O'Brien, and Clemm looked at Jennifer.

"I mean, you just said it, Marty. Talk was all Albert Brady and the other two had ever been about as far as anyone could tell. Skirmishes here and there with neighbors and authorities for creating nuisances in public places with their religious tirades. But at the end of the day, it was all still just talk."

Clemm said, "In fact, the three were officially ruled to have been acting alone in the Beardsly bombing. But I've always thought that just isn't likely. They seemed to have slid into the school too smoothly, first with the demolitions work, then with the actual walk-in and takeover."

"But we didn't have a reason to single Amory out then," Sean joined in. "We didn't have a reason to suspect he could have been working with the terrorists."

"But why didn't hindsight prompt a closer look?"
Clemm asked. "Not just at Amory, I mean in general.
I'm not criticizing, Sean, but it seems to me the bureau would have pushed harder to determine for
sure that those three terrorists were the only ones
involved. The bureau had to figure the public would
want to definitively know."

"Except you're forgetting a key element to all of
that missing zeal, Bob."

Clemm waited, looking impatient.

"The children were already dead. All of the postmortem in the world wasn't going to mitigate that
factor, or the fact that the bureau assigned to save
their lives had botched up."

Jennifer heard Sean's personal condemnation. Before she'd met him, she would have concurred. Now
that she was beginning to know him, she hated to
hear that self-judgment from a good man who obviously cared.

No one seemed eager to resume conversation immediately, so they went back to the files until
O'Brien said, "Well, here's another link. Amory is
slowly but surely losing his elusiveness the more
we dig."

"What do you have?" Sean leaned forward.

O'Brien handed him a single sheet of paper.

Sean held one of the lists of dead, with their corresponding photos. Then his eyes backed up to a name and a face as realization hit.

"What?" Jennifer took the paper from Sean's hands to see what had caused his eyes to go so curiously dark. She scanned down the page before she saw it, too.

Among the dead was an eight-year-old boy. She'd seen his face just a few moments ago. Where—? She searched through a discarded stack of papers and picked up a news photo. It was the same boy. Same first name, by which he was identified only in the photo. And suddenly, an explanation for the man who hugged him, for his look of devotion she'd thought excessive toward a mere student.

Roy Amory had lived that day because he'd not been in the building. But a little boy *had* been in the building that day, seemingly in perfect health despite the developmental handicap that had marked his short life.

In Samuel Amory, the Beardsly school had lost one among other innocent victims. In the "Sam" of the photo, Roy Amory, clearly his father, had lost his son.

It was the second night he'd been here and still nothing. Roy wasn't coming home.

Ben Keaghan bypassed Roy's house and headed for a final turn around the block. Even though it was still shy of eight p.m., most of the houses in this upscale neighborhood were dark.

The yuppies and older professionals who lived here were winding down in their back bedrooms or dens before turning in early. Had to be well-rested so that they could wake up alert, primed to earn those admirable salaries after surviving the stress of their early-morning bumper-to-bumper commutes.

Ben knew that to look at him, most people would visually slot his clean-cut looks in the same category. Which was probably why no one had called the police on him, if they'd bothered to wonder why a well-heeled tan sport sedan was cruising through the neighborhood for the second night in a row.

His renting the car had been essential. If police bulletins had been issued for him, clearly they had to be searching for his sport utility truck. It sat in a field off some beaten path now, stripped of its license plate, which he carried in this car's trunk.

Ben drove on, thinking how the neighbors would all blanch if they could read any of the thoughts on his mind. They'd quail if they knew the absolute malice he bore one of their own—a nondescript computer analyst whose luck was running out. Because Ben held Roy's rope.

He didn't know, realistically, how long he could

elude the police. A few hours ago, he'd heard that first bulletin "requesting" his presence for questioning. He'd even debated very briefly going in, cutting some deal that favored him in exchange for his giving them the information they wanted on Roy.

But the memory of Judy and Hal's faces as they'd been that night in the cabin when all of this had sounded so easy and the kidnapping was still yet to be kept him on the road. He never should have gotten involved in all of this. He never should have mentioned to Judy that Lattimore sometimes shopped in his furniture store. Never should have given that opening to her to give to Roy.

But he had. He'd even helped Judy talk Hal into joining the kidnapping scheme for all that lovely money it promised.

Now he wanted Roy for himself. The law, no matter how harsh, wouldn't give him the satisfaction of revenge he craved. Even his anticipation of the money, of having his ample share, was starting to fade. Realistically, the authorities were closing in so that it looked like that just wasn't going to happen either.

But Roy could still die. And if he was staying away from this house, he had to be holing up somewhere at night after he left work. Wherever he kept the boy.

Where he contemplated life after the boy's death. Or by now, was he thinking of his own? He himself had always sensed that in Roy—the death wish. It was a weakness in his character that always, even to the end probably, seemed to elude Judy.

Well, Roy would have his wish. Ben would see to it. And he'd go back to the cheap room he was renting under his assumed name tonight. Tomorrow, he'd beat Roy to work to make sure he showed up there. Then later, he'd trail him home, wherever that was, to end the series of killings so ignominiously launched by this whole ill-begotten Charlie Lattimore affair.

The cop on the late shift started paying attention to the caller when she threw out Ben's name.

"Ma'am, I'm sorry, I didn't quite get that. You say you have knowledge of Ben Keaghan's whereabouts?"

"Well I screwed him last night, I ought to know," the prostitute answered indignantly.

"Where are you calling from, ma'am?"

"A motel off the downtown strip. That doesn't matter. What does is, Ben Keaghan's here in town, not down in Southern Indiana like that news report I just watched speculated."

"Did he tell you where he was headed?"

"He just paid his money and left."

"Any chance you remember what he was driving?"

The prostitute chuckled.

The cop just sighed.

The prostitute said, "Okay, but seriously—the answer's no. I mean not specifically, I'm not good at cars. Besides, the lights on the street where we met weren't exactly lit up for surveillance, you see."

"Okay, ma'am, we appreciate the tip."

"Hey, don't hang up yet! Don't I get a reward?"

"Sir, I hope I haven't disturbed your evening, but you did leave your number, and this is important." Jennifer interpreted the beat of silence from Devlin Thompson as his wondering why she'd summoned him and not Anthony Collins at half past nine at night.

"You're not disturbing me, Agent Bennett. I'm well aware of the kidnapper's demands."

Jennifer crossed her legs where she sat perched on the side of her hotel bed. "Yes, that's precisely why I'm calling, to request copies of some of the profile reports compiled during the Beardsly case. In addition to the one for Albert Brady, I'm specifically interested in material that targets local religious extremists."

"Any particular group you have in mind?"

"I'd like feedback on all that were investigated. And I'll tell you, in light of what we've turned up on Amory, I'd especially appreciate any information on those with a connection to or fixation on children."

"Does Sean know you're making this request?"

Jennifer hesitated. "Not yet."

"Why not? He's your superior on this."

Jennifer took exception to his tone. "Oh? I thought you'd pegged Collins for that."

"No need for sarcasm, Agent Bennett. You know what I mean."

"And *you* know I'm not speaking out of line."

Thompson didn't reply at first. Then very softly, he murmured, "All right. You'll have your reports by morning. Good night."

"Good night." She waited for him to hang up first. Then she sat down on her bed, gazing around her very nice room, reflecting on the liberty she'd just taken.

Why *had* she made the request? Jennifer answered herself with a mental sniff. She knew exactly why she'd made it.

Because of Sean Alexander's face as she'd last seen it tonight.

Before O'Brien and Clemm had left, they'd all agreed they absolutely could not let this kidnapping resolve on Roy Amory's terms. Because by six p.m.

tomorrow afternoon, Charlie Lattimore would probably be dead.

Which meant they had to find a way to force the resolution. Which meant they had to find Amory and reclaim the boy. Even now, warrants were being sought to search Roy Amory's home. O'Brien and Clemm were grabbing the last bit of rest they'd probably be able to get before morning.

At that time, they planned to go back to Amory's firm to do the interviews with friends and colleagues, which would hopefully yield some insight to his absence from work and possible whereabouts.

As all of this planning was being made, Sean had contributed to the discussion only as necessary. When he hadn't been contributing, he'd appeared distant and very quiet. Too quiet, Jennifer thought. And she could guess it was the guilt over not only the entire Beardsly loss, but now also the particular death of a grief-driven man who had lost his only son.

"Do you want to talk about it before you go home?" Jennifer had asked him after the other two agents had left. Sean had looked up from the cleared conference room table into her face, as if surprised she, too, was still sitting there.

"There's nothing to talk about, Jennifer. Everything that needs to be said has already been discussed."

"Sean, clearly the man is grieving, and clearly his

pain is a pitiful thing. But no amount of personal anguish can condone the crime he's chosen to commit in order to act out his misplaced anger."

"Unacceptable as his feelings may be, Jennifer, they're not entirely misplaced. Maybe if we hadn't hesitated to act more forcefully things would have turned out differently. Maybe if the negotiating had just ended when the hostage guys failed to reach Brady, if I hadn't intervened and prolonged the kidnappers' option of killing those children, they would still be alive today."

She hadn't known how to respond, because her gut reaction to what he said left her more than a little off balance. They were Sean Alexander's words, but she could have been looking at—and listening to—herself talking. Didn't his hawkish second-guessing reflect what she'd shared with other bureau colleagues about his performance herself?

Yet hearing it now, in light of how she'd seen how deeply Sean cared and carried that commitment through in his professionalism, she couldn't help thinking Sean was wrong. Yes, his team and the hostage specialists could have forced their adversaries' hand earlier and possibly prevailed. But given those men's frame of mind, Jennifer thought the likelihood of loss of life would have been not just a possibility, but a definite probability.

Sean Alexander should have prevailed that day.

Those children should have lived because the approach he took to diffuse their abductors was appropriate, all of his moves right.

So why *hadn't* he won? Hence her call to Devlin Thompson to help find her that answer. Because she *had* considered enlisting Collins as an ally in her quest—and rejected him in favor of a man who truly considered himself Sean's friend. Anthony Collins had revealed to her that he was working from an agenda he believed would help the bureau. But Jennifer had sensed from the start he was just as clearly still grinding an ax against Sean.

And even beyond that, perhaps the bottom line was, Collins didn't work in the field. She did and so did Sean. Collins couldn't begin to understand, from behind his desk, the human details that shaped, altered, and dictated professional decisions they and agents like them had to make at a moment's notice.

And in that conference room tonight, she'd searched for words to relay the empathy she felt on that point to Sean. She'd wanted to let him know that for the first time in her career, seeing someone struggle with that dilemma—seeing him struggle—was making her reevaluate the merit of her own ideas about caution. Not weakness, as some uninformed outsiders might judge, but measured thought.

"You should get some sleep, too," Sean had finally

told her. Then he'd stood to leave himself. "When that warrant comes in, I'll call you."

She'd nodded, still seeking encouraging words beyond textbook platitudes common to the job. But Sean had already turned to go. And soon after that, the conference room door was clicking decisively behind him.

Jennifer got off the bed now, knowing she should be lying down. But she was still restless. Despite her body's fatigue, she just wasn't ready for sleep. Maybe she'd indulge herself as she too rarely did lately. She'd seek out the anonymous company of strangers in the still-open lounge downstairs. She'd order something hot and soothing to drink that would help her reflect and think.

She grabbed her purse off the dresser, unchained and unlocked her door, then checked her dress pocket for her room key.

Touching the coded card, she swung open the door and nearly ran into Sean.

He shouldn't have come up here he'd thought all the way up the elevator, then all the way down the hall to her room. He knew it as soon as he raised his hand to knock on her door and she intercepted, stepping back, startled.

He knew it as soon as her expression turned hesitant, reminiscent of that other time he'd made an advance, before easing into something expectant and soft. He was sure of it as he stood there wanting to respond to that softness while every thought about Beardsly she'd invited him to share—which he'd finally admitted his *need* to share on his way home—went out of his head.

What registered instead was that it was late, she wasn't shutting him out, and he stood here wanting something. Inner peace. A space of forgetfulness. A comforting spirit that *understood*, even if it didn't approve or condone. A soothing presence who walked the walk every day as he did and, in so doing, simply understood.

And when Jennifer hesitantly extended a hand to him with a gently questioning, "Sean?" he also knew the rest. At this moment, neither their professional nor personal differences mattered. She embodied the spirit he craved. At this moment, more than anything, Sean wanted *her*.

Jennifer saw it in his eyes. The hesitant question, the reluctant vulnerability, the unspoken need. From the first, she'd sensed the emotional threat he posed to her self-possession. From the first, she had defensively lashed out at it, which meant lashing out at him until the reality of the man intruded and eroded her determination to fight.

And so now it was coming down to her and him, without the parameters of their job, without social implications, without considerations each imposed on them both. It came down to her admitting to herself that Sean Alexander was an unexpected kindred spirit wrapped in gentle strength that, at this moment, he was offering to her. And she wanted it.

She didn't withdraw her hand. Rather, she extended it until her fingers touched his hand, which still rested at his side. Then he slowly reciprocated by turning the contact palm to palm, by letting his fingers firmly entwine with hers.

After that, there was only the soft click of the door behind Sean as she closed it after drawing him inside. She'd already turned one of the two lamps in the room off when she'd prepared to leave for downstairs. So now, their way was illuminated by little more than the soft light from a small table lamp at the far end of the room. Its spill barely reached to the space where they stood, and where he drew her into his arms softly and bent his head to kiss her.

Jennifer sighed as he moved even closer and slid one hand leisurely up from her waist, over the contouring line of her back, to her nape before moving a fraction more to sink into the fullness of her hair. Her lips parted on a little breath at the easy sensuality of his movement. Sean immediately took advantage by deepening their kiss. He teased her with tugging nips of his teeth against her mouth, then with the softness of his tongue, tasting the moist heat that had gathered there.

His soft aggression encouraged Jennifer to move in closer to explore. She slipped her hands inside his open suit jacket to push it up and off his shoulders. It fell to their feet in a whisper of cloth on the floor. She let her hands roam without direction across the broad expanse of his back. She smiled when he brought his lips to the side of her neck, shivering a little while she let her hands roam some more.

And then she shivered when he shifted his hands to the top of the long zipper of her dress. Slowly, he lowered it. Just as leisurely, he brought his mouth back to hers. He kissed her deeply then and slid his fingers into the open panels at the base of her back. The sides of the dress slipped a little more, off her shoulders, to partially catch on Sean's forearms and the skin of his hair-dusted wrists.

He stretched the moment, letting the fabric move with him as he fondled the skin he touched. Clearly savoring, he inspired Jennifer to want to savor too, especially when he broke their kiss to whisper against her chin, "I won't mind if you touch, too."

That made Jennifer smile and step back to let the dress fall fully. And then she lost her smile as Sean reached out to touch her and strip from her the silken undergarments that joined her clothes on the floor. She kept watching him as she unbuttoned his shirt. Then she pulled it from his pants and removed it, and felt a little rush of excitement when he dropped his arms to his sides, inviting her to do whatever, as long as it was more.

She was leaning forward to kiss him, but was almost startled when Sean suddenly reached out to take her hand in a soft but not quite gentle hold. She lost her breath when he resumed the kiss and made it hotter for them both by placing her hand where he wanted it to go. Not breaking their contact, he walked her backward to the bed and lowered her, then removed his trousers and briefs before joining her there.

Then they were moving together, and Jennifer could only think of how gloriously hard he was where she was so soft. He was gentle and he was tough. He was everything in this moment Jennifer had always most wanted a lover to be. Fully there for her, asking in husky murmurs what she wanted, what she needed. Demanding for himself in a lover-roughened voice, with a touch, a sound, or sometimes just a kiss, what he needed in return.

Until finally she could only feel . . . his hands at her waist . . . his tongue at her breasts . . . his warm heavy legs shifting with hers then parting them, asking her permission even now for the joining they so badly wanted.

She breathed shallowly against his throat, girl-like wonder mingling with urgent gratitude as he groaned and, at last, pressed deep, deep inside of her. Her hands curved around his shoulders, and the blunted ends of her short nails clenched against his skin.

She shifted her legs beneath his, feeling his hard thrusts at the very core of her body. She was going up too fast without him, but was unable to temper her response to this pleasure he gave.

And so she shut her eyes and held him, and concentrated fiercely on the sensation. His breathing became uneven, his slipping control moved him higher and more sharply against her, driving single-mindedly for more.

Then suddenly she gasped, "Sean!" and arched as the tension inside her peaked.

Sean was trembling, but he went still on outstretched arms above her. Jennifer drew his head down and lifted a little at the same time to capture his trembling lips with a kiss. Then suddenly, he thrust compulsively against her once, twice, again, while his body shuddered in a fierce grip.

When it was over, he sank heavily upon her, and Jennifer thought his weight should have been too much. But, as had everything else they'd so unexpectedly shared between them tonight, even the intimacy of that felt right.

Inevitably, however, their bodies had to cool. And as they did, Jennifer grew apprehensive of the rationalizations calmer reasoning would surely compel either of them, or both, to make. She didn't want to express or hear any of it. She didn't want what she had just experienced with Sean to be explained away.

She just wanted to hold their lovemaking close to her heart, close to that place he had unwittingly breached from the first. And maybe more than that, she wanted to believe that Sean wanted the same, or that at least he felt moved enough to postpone any postmortem until the heated memory of it all could stand the sort of dissection waiting in the colder light of day.

Long, long moments drifted by, and Sean said nothing. But neither did he take his arms from around her or make a move to leave her side. With an inward sigh, Jennifer thought ruefully, what a precious pair they must make. Fearless in the face of peril or even death in a job that routinely pitted them against the most dangerous criminals. Yet here they lay, as timid as children to express or even explore what their bodies had just shown them could come to matter to their hearts.

"Sean—" Jennifer wasn't sure what she wanted to say. Maybe she just wanted to be reassured by his voice.

"Don't," he replied, and placed his fingers under her chin to bring her face around for a tender kiss. "Just let me hold you."

Jennifer did, content for now, wary of the tenuous

sound of his plea. Only time would give them the answers they sought, she supposed. For right now, she curled into Sean and let the sleep that beckoned them both gently claim her.

Chapter Thirteen

Day Five

The shrill of the phone from her side of the bed woke her. Jennifer looked at the clock beside it—two-fifty-seven a.m.—before she picked up. "Yes, hello?"

"Agent Bennett, I'm sorry to get you out of bed." Jennifer listened to Devlin Thompson's apology and involuntarily looked over her shoulder at Sean. He was on his back with his arms under his head, staring at the ceiling, listening to what she would say into the phone.

"The materials you requested are going to be messengered to the field office there by no later than six this morning," Thompson continued. "But that's not the most urgent news I have for you."

Jennifer turned away from Sean and his questioning look at her prolonged silence to better concentrate on what Thompson was saying. "What news do you have, sir?"

"Someone I was checking out who seems to fit within the guidelines of what you wanted. He shares an unusual religious affiliation with Roy Amory. His name is Phillip Belamy, and he's being flown into Indianapolis this morning. You and Sean need to talk to him when he's delivered to headquarters there."

Jennifer felt the mattress shift and turned. Sean was sitting on the edge of the bed. His back was to her, but clearly he was still intent on what she was saying. "We'll be there to receive both the report and the man. Thanks for the call." Only at the pause on the other end of the phone did she realize how intimate she'd unconsciously made the referenced "we" sound. She silently swore at her lapse. Perhaps Thompson would take it in the general sense.

"How is Sean?"

Or perhaps not. "He's well. Do you have a message for me to pass on to him when I see him?" She listened to another nonresponse.

"No, no message. You can still grab a couple of hours' rest, Agent Bennett. Go back to bed. Sleep well." He hung up.

Bastard, Jennifer thought, hanging up, too.

"Who was it?" Sean asked.

Jennifer thought though the question wasn't unexpected, his tone sounded a little gruff. He'd probably become sterner still after she told him. "Devlin Thompson." She shifted to her side and propped herself up against the pillows. She also brought the sheet she and Sean had climbed under at some point during the night up under her arms as he swiveled partially around. "He's calling you here at this hour? At your hotel?"

Jennifer sighed and dived in. "I called him yesterday, Sean, to ask him a favor. He was reporting back to me that what I asked has been done."

His voice still mild, Sean wanted to know, "And that favor was?"

"After our meeting with O'Brien and Clemm last night, a portion of the conversation kept going through my mind. It was when we were questioning why those three terrorists at Beardsly would have actually gone through with something as literal as blowing up the school when they had never individually or collectively done anything so violent before."

Sean turned enough to bring one leg back upon the bed. "Obviously discarding the theory that there's a first time for everything, what did you decide?"

Jennifer frowned a little, not entirely trusting his apparent calm. "I asked Thompson to send a compilation of more information to us that profiled known religious extremists—both groups and individuals—around the time just before and leading up to the bombing. I have a hunch something could lead back to Amory."

Sean studied her. "Were you going to share this with me anytime soon?"

"Sean—"

"Or were you just going to spring it on me if and when you decided it panned out? By the way, why did you call Thompson with this instead—"

"Don't you say it! It's exactly because I knew you'd fly off like this, because you'd insist on interpreting what I'd done in exactly this wrong way.

"The truth, Agent Alexander, is that I just didn't want the obstruction of that. We don't have the luxury of the sort of time it requires to duke it out over turf. Though you still won't admit it, you're still too vulnerable about California in ways that are mostly detrimental to yourself. And now, with what we've learned about Roy Amory's involvement, I was afraid that sentiment would just turn worse."

"So you're saying you've decided I can't handle this, is that it?"

His voice was as cutting as jagged ice. "Sean, please, I don't want to fight!" Jennifer dropped her head and ran a weary hand over her eyes. "Especially not now," she added more quietly and looked back up at him. He was turned away now so that all she could see by the moonlight that limned the room was his handsome stubborn profile.

She tried again. "We're relatively certain Roy Amory is our abductor, yes. But we need to know why in order to understand how he's working this, and where he's possibly hiding out. Once we know that, we'll be closer to a position of strength to bargain for Charlie's life if it actually comes to that."

Sean reached down to pick his clothes up from the floor. He stood, and Jennifer caught a glimpse of his taut backside before he stepped into his pants and walked away from the bed. Beside the window, he drew a panel of the white sheers partially aside and stood there for long moments, looking out in contemplative silence.

"Of course I'm not suggesting you can't handle this, Sean," Jennifer said. "More than you can know, I increasingly find myself convinced that no one but you could have been more right to negotiate that situation. But I also stand by the claim I just made. Pathos is a pitiful thing, but when it comes to Amory, you may be assigning him a degree of it that's inappropriate. And that may be blindsiding you to options that may not be as cut-and-dried as you've convinced yourself they've got to be."

"You mean Roy Amory and this possible extremist link you've alerted Thompson to and rightfully reminded me we're obligated to investigate." Now he turned to her. "I wasn't angry with you a moment ago, Jennifer. I was angry with myself. Charlie Lattimore deserves the best I have to give. And it stung to know I needed a swift kick in the ass from an agent I respect to remember that."

Jennifer didn't know what to say. He'd disarmed her again.

Sean dropped the curtain and walked back to where she sat, still propped against the headboard. Sitting so close his thigh touched hers through the sheet, he cupped her face and leaned in to give her a brief kiss. Then he leaned away again, letting his thumbs caress her jaw. "I mean it, I'm not blaming you. You've reached some conclusions, and they're no more than what I should have been telling myself for almost a year instead of mourning something I couldn't change."

"Don't think I'm trivializing what you went through, Sean. That's the last thing I want to do."

"I know. But I wasn't so sure when you showed up that first time at Lattimore's estate all bristly and beautiful and ready to, in some way I couldn't figure, do me in."

Jennifer dropped her eyes from his. With an aimless finger, she plucked at the sheet. She wondered how she could have gotten so far into her adult life to only now meet a man who, with the sheer force of his patience, so completely unnerved her.

Sean, noting her pensiveness, lifted her chin. "Is something the matter? Tell me what it is."

Dammit why was she feeling close to tears? "Do you really think I'm beautiful?" she surprised herself by saying. She raised her eyes, looking for the truth and got a smile. Sean looked at her in a very male way. The faint grooves in his cheeks deepened, heightening her nerves.

"Listen to me, Jennifer. Whatever happens from this moment forward, I can tell you now with a fair degree of certainty that about this," he leaned forward to kiss her brow, then leaned away to touch her chin and hold her eyes, "I don't have any regrets."

"I wasn't fishing . . ."

"Yes you were," he contradicted mildly. "And it's all right though unnecessary. I came here to your room needing something even I didn't realize I was looking for until you helped me glimpse it tonight."

"What?"

Sean pressed his fingers against her lips. "It's better left for later. Just tell me one thing right now."

She brought her hand up to lightly clasp one of his wrists. "What?" she asked again.

"Are you going to run away from this when it's all just a memory? What happened here tonight?"

He wasn't asking a literal question. She knew they both had a great deal of thinking to do. But at least, he was saying they might agree to try. "No," she answered, "I won't run."

Sean smiled, but it was slight. Jennifer could already sense the myriad of thoughts turning inside his head. But she could also see in the directness of his eyes that when those questions settled, the quiet place they had found here together in this room would resurface. And when it did, she wouldn't necessarily have anything dire to fear.

Out of the silence, a pulsing beep broke the still air. Jennifer jumped a little before she realized what it was. Sean let her go and walked around to the other side of the bed to retrieve his suit jacket. From an inner pocket he pulled out his beeper. He punched in the number then sat back down on the bed and motioned to Jennifer for the phone.

She stretched the cord across her chest and handed it to him.

He only waited a moment after punching in the number to say, "Alexander." He listened. "You pulled him out of bed at this hour, I'm sure he was pissed. But what did he say?" He listened again. "All right. Agent Bennett and I will be there."

He hung up. "That was the prosecutor. The judge granting our warrant for Amory's premises will see that it's processed and ready to go in a couple of hours. We need to be downtown as soon as it's ready to pick up."

Jennifer looked at the clock again. It was three-thirty a.m.

*　　*　　*

Charlie couldn't sleep. For hours he'd lain awake, afraid to close his eyes, afraid that if he did the man would creep down the stairs and see to it that he never opened them again.

Because the man couldn't sleep either. Charlie heard his heavy footsteps above the basement ceiling, walking back and forth across the kitchen floor, as he had been doing since late last night.

The window Charlie had worked so hard to uncover was nailed over with several planks of heavy wood now. His second fiercest enemy was the series of nails the man had angrily pounded in place to ensure his victim didn't accidently find a way to escape again.

Charlie looked at his watch by the glow of the lamp. Four fifteen in the morning. What would happen when it came time for the man to leave for work? Would he come down those steps and kill him then? Or would he just decide to stick to the routine—feed him and then leave?

Charlie sighed wishing that for just a few moments, he could sleep. He wished the man would sleep, too. But instead, the footsteps continued to clack back and forth across the kitchen floor. In an almost detached way, Charlie started to wonder, was the man trying to figure out the best way to kill his hostage?

*　　*　　*

Ben Keaghan double-checked the clip in his pistol. Should he head out to the firm and put himself into position while it was still dark, he wondered? He drew aside a corner of his motel room curtain, looking two stories down to the moon-dappled roofs of the cheap cars dotting the parking lot.

Or should he wait until there was a little light outside? By doing that, he would draw less attention to himself in case there was anyone—especially a cop—in the mood to notice a lone car cruising the vicinity of a modest suburban engineering business. Especially at a time when there wouldn't possibly be any employees inside.

Ben sat in the room's single chair. He laid his gun in his lap. Then he proceeded to think and stare at the dark screen of the dilapidated television sagging on his dresser. It looked as if management had reclaimed it from one of the trash heaps in the alley outside.

He'd wait until it got light, but just barely. He wasn't sure what time the place opened or when Roy's shift started. But he didn't want to miss that man no matter how early he showed up.

The clock on the car dash read five forty-five by the time Sean and Jennifer left the downtown government building. Search warrant in hand, they headed for the northside suburb and the last known recorded residence of Roy Amory.

Commuter traffic was negligible. Even when it picked up, the heaviest flow of it would be traveling opposite Jennifer and Sean to interstate arteries leading downtown or to major through streets that spilled into any number of the surrounding suburban office complexes.

Within minutes, Sean and Jennifer entered the tidy cul-de-sac community and quickly found Roy's house. It was a two-story gray brick with a spacious two-car garage and expansive front lawn. The lawn was covered with enough unraked leaves to present a pretty welcome mat that, nonetheless, was incongruous to the immaculately raked lawns of his neighbors.

As Jennifer and Sean parked in the drive, they could see by the moon, which still hadn't made way for the autumn sun, that no lights were on in the house.

"Do you think he's here anyway?" Jennifer asked. "Doesn't look like it."

Sean's hand was on his door. "Let's get inside."

They knocked on the front door. No lights clicked on to greet them. No footsteps could be heard in the entryway on the other side of the door. No voice, irritated at being roused this early in the morning, could be heard approaching either.

Sean picked the lock with a minimum amount of noise, then they were inside.

Jennifer flipped on the foyer light. A flagstone entryway led off in three directions. One of their options was to follow the entry straight across to the foot of a staircase. Another was to turn right into what looked like a formal dining room. Their third was to turn left into what looked like a very well-stocked library. That room featured two floor-to-ceiling cases of books, but other than that, a very modest sofa, coffee table and end chair.

As they studied things to their right, Jennifer and Sean saw that the dining room had the same odd appointment. The table and chairs were plain. Jennifer began to guess how a man of modest means, as Roy Amory's tax records documented him to be, could afford such a home.

He couldn't and was pouring most of the salary he made into his mortgage rather than costly furnishings for his impressive house.

They decided to take the stairs first. On the second-floor landing were two bedrooms with a full master bath off one, a half-bath off the other. And there was another meagerly furnished room that was the den. Inside the bedroom with the half-bath, Jennifer spotted a toy collection—stuffed animals and miniature promotional figures, many of which were characters from movies already best remembered as yesterday's sensation.

And there were books. Even with a gap at the end of one bookcase, the quantity was impressive. They were mostly picture books featuring young heroic boys fighting fantastic technicolor foes.

And finally, most fascinatingly, there were pictures of Samuel Amory. In some, he was alone in a yard with a small black dog. In most, he was standing with Amory and a woman who, from the way she was included in their embrace on a beach, Jennifer presumed to be Samuel's mother.

While Jennifer was methodically searching that room, Sean took the master bedroom at the end of hall. He came up with the same results, nothing. He decided to start downstairs while Jennifer finished off the upper level with a search of the den and a tiny utility closet under an alcove beside the stairs.

What she found did nothing to change her mind. Sparse furnishings were all Roy Amory had up here. No hostage or any indication that there ever had been anyone here seemed evident. Except for the little boy who lived in Roy Amory's mind.

She joined Sean downstairs. As she walked into the library, where he was going through the drawer of the coffee table, he said, "You know what this house is starting to feel like? A prop in a movie, a stage set. Only the bare minimum of personal items to make it livable."

"Yeah," Jennifer agreed. "And even those things have the feel of a false front when you look closely. Did you do the dining room yet?"

"Be my guest. I'm almost done here, then I'll get the kitchen."

Twenty minutes later, they were still as empty-handed as they'd been when they'd arrived. All that was left was the garage. A common door in the kitchen closed off that space, which they accessed by climbing down a shallow set of steps.

They didn't actually need to get to the bottom to see that perhaps, again, they were about to get lucky.

From his study phone, Paul Lattimore said to his lawyer, "Are we on track with that money? I need it by no later than four, you know that."

"Are you sure you want to do this, Paul? You told me yourself the authorities have advised you against it."

"They're not the ones trying to get any children of theirs back alive. If something goes wrong with their plan, I want to be prepared to give that son-of-a-bitch holding Charlie exactly what he's asked for. If I have to, *I'll* even take it."

The lawyer's sigh was heartfelt. "I strongly urge

you to rethink this, Paul. You've trusted them this far. Keep taking their advice."

"You're saying you're refusing to carry out my request, is that it?"

"No. Of course I'll arrange to have the funds transferred to your bank if that's what you really want."

"Thanks."

"Don't thank me yet until this all turns out. Wait for my call. And while you're waiting, Paul, *think.*"

"Either Amory's taken up a hobby as a survivalist, or he's spent a lot of money and care on preparing for a prolonged confinement," Jennifer observed.

They were wading through boxes, cartons, and smaller containers, now empty, that had previously contained quantities of functional housewares—none of which were evident in the house they had just exited. According to the evidence they found in Roy Amory's two-car garage, they should have been wading through scads of electrical equipment, lumber, appliance parts, and cookware.

"Let's talk to some neighbors," Sean suggested, "see if they know where Amory is."

After knocking on the two doors flanking Amory's house, Sean and Jennifer's combined neighborly consensus was the same. About two months ago, Roy Amory had talked about taking a vacation. A camping trip, he said, somewhere in the wilds of Michigan. Except to insist how he looked forward to it, he hadn't told them much else. Not even when he expected to be back home.

Jennifer and Sean thanked them and walked back down the trim crushed brick driveway to leave. As Sean was backing out, Jennifer punched in the number to downtown headquarters. She asked the receptionist to put her through to Arty Hopkins.

"Arty, we need some checks run fast. Can you see if Amory's name turns up with any auto shops around the city? See if he paid any of them a visit for recent tune-ups or repairs. Check the travel agencies, too, to see if he's made any out-of-state travel plans. Concentrate on backroad styled arrangements. And put Michigan at the top of your destination list."

"Anything else?"

"Sean and I are on our way back, and we'll take this next part over from you if you'll start it. We need to look at property rentals or leases that might have been recently issued to Amory of course, but more likely to someone whose name may be similar to that. The focus should be a country location since that's the reference Judy Keaghan cites in her diary."

"Okay. What else?"

"Before you start on any of that, contact community relations to tell them it's time to put the word out over the public airwaves. We're calling it. Roy

Amory is to be apprehended and brought in on sight."

"It's done."

There was nothing on the radio, Roy was thinking ten minutes later. Not even about Ben. Nothing on the television, either. In fact, news about the kidnapping in general, with the exception of retread about what the media already knew, hadn't changed.

Did that mean whatever leads they had were drying up? That whatever trail or trails they'd been sniffing were turning cold?

Did it mean fortune had granted him one last window of opportunity? Today was it. After today, there would be no going back. Not to his present life as he knew it, which he had to start thinking of as his old life now. Not to the existence he'd imagined when he'd conceived, so long ago, this entire kidnapping plot.

Which was why he needed a talisman to cheer him on. A momento of faith that he foolishly had left at his office inside his desk drawer, so that he would always feel sweet Sam still by his side.

He needed the lock of hair he had cut from Sam's head with his own hands for the very first time. Sam's mother had laughed, teasing Roy for doing a lopsided job. But Sam had looked adorable anyway. The three of them had gone to the beach to frolic and play because those were the years when Roy's life had been sunshine.

His wife still had two years to live before the drunk driver who killed her struck. And Charlie, whose parents thought him charmingly fey, had yet to be diagnosed as developmentally disabled. It would just be three short years before he embarked down the road that altered his young life.

The hair was a reminder, Roy thought as he paced and stroked his jaw with his pistol. More than that, God had told him that on this day of all days, Roy needed it in his hands in order to receive His divine sign.

He didn't have a choice. He had to go back into work once last time to retrieve the last physical reminder of his boy. He'd just have to be extremely careful, be on his guard looking out for men like those two in the sedan yesterday. Looking out for cops.

Roy slipped the pistol inside the kitchen utility drawer. He'd retrieve it in time for this evening for Agent Jennifer Bennett, who was going to make his money drop.

Roy Amory checked his tie in the reflection of the refrigerator door, zipped up his windbreaker, and walked out his kitchen.

Chapter Fourteen

Ten a.m.

Jennifer thought Phillip Belamy looked more like an accountant than what he was, what her grandfather would call a jack-legged preacher. She and Sean sat opposite the man, who was dressed as professionally and conservatively as they were. A conference room table separated them.

Belamy had been delivered just thirty minutes ago from his Santa Barbara home to this Indianapolis FBI field office because, he told them, he had been encouraged to cooperate fully, or else. The nature of what else, it turned out, was vulnerability to a conspiracy charge to commit a federal crime.

So now, Jennifer and Sean were allowing Hopkins to get a headstart on the rental property search while they sat watching Belamy lean back with his borrowed coffee mug and talk expansively.

"I knew Roy Amory was crazy five minutes after I met him in my church in L.A.," Belamy boasted. "But what the hell, lots of people are crazy. Doesn't mean they'll necessarily harm you."

"What did you say your church was, Mr. Belamy?" Sean asked.

"The Church of The One. God, you understand, who is the true and only One. Everything begins and ends with Him, all the little children of the world are spirits born to be showered in His beautiful sun."

Sean just looked at him. "I see. You say harmless is the impression you immediately formed of Amory? That he didn't seem to project either menace or threat?"

"No, he was too devoted to his little family for that. A mousy little wife and their son. Unfortunate about the boy, turned out he was retarded or something."

The sensitivity of a snake, Jennifer was thinking. "And you knew Roy Amory for how long?"

"Oh, he attended my church for about a year, I guess. Very discreetly within that time span. He was sensitive to how our unorthodox views might have unsettled his superiors at his school. You do know he was a vice principal at an elementary school, don't you?"

Jennifer said, "Yes."

"I always thought it was Brady who corrupted him—"

"Albert Brady?" Sean interrupted. "What do you mean?"

"Albert was a deacon in my church when Roy joined. But right around the time Roy's wife died, Albert took a few of my followers and segmented off into a sect of his own. It was a group who took our core beliefs to radical extremes."

"Extremes that advocated harm to those who didn't adhere to the beliefs of the church in total?" Sean asked, to clarify.

"Yes, which ultimately threatened harm to the very children my church, as it was founded, encouraged followers to revere. Amory and his wife were both affiliated with the Beardsly school by the time Roy joined the church. His wife thought our teachings were nonsense, but Roy, in his own way, was devout."

"You were sure of this because?" Jennifer prompted.

"Oh, we used to have long talks about it. You see, before he branched off with Brady, he used to worry that in pursuing his affiliation with Beardsly and attending to the needs of his own son through them, he was somehow violating the spirit of the tenants of this church. He feared he was living a lie. Worse, he feared he was encouraging his only son to live a lie."

"Which made it easier for Albert Brady to exercise his influence over Amory and to bring him around to his way of believing."

"I still didn't think anything came of Brady's trying until one day I overheard him and Amory in the church vestibule talking. They were trying to decide something about a gun. I was curious, so I concealed myself a little closer to the conversation.

"It turned out, and I didn't realize this until much later, that they were talking about Beardsly. Brady said something about two others in the congregation having expertise with explosives, and that's when Roy Amory answered with something I couldn't make out about guns."

"You didn't think to report this to the police?" Jennifer was incredulous.

"You have to understand something, Agent Bennett, something I alluded to before. Roy Amory was prone to exaggeration. And Albert Brady was a loudmouth who had never so much as actually swatted a fly in my presence. Given that, what should I have been thinking? That this wasn't one of their typical crackpot conversations? That they were serious all of a sudden?"

"They were," Sean pointed out.

"Yes, despite what you obviously think about me, detectives, I am sorry about that. After it was all over—well, it was done. I only wished I hadn't learned about the explosives too late."

Sean looked at Jennifer. "What do you mean, learned about explosives? What did you discover later that you didn't know then?"

"Why, that Roy was the point man, of course."

Jennifer shot a look at Sean. He had gone still too. "*Roy* was the point man?"

"Yes, Agent Alexander. Unbeknownst to Brady, one of the two men on the inside, the two who coordinated the demolitions, was paid off by Roy to create a duplicate detonation device prior to that explosion. Roy feared some glitch just like what happened would go down."

"That being?" Jennifer pressed.

"Roy feared at the end that Brady would lose his nerve, like he usually did. Roy feared that at the critical moment in their scheme, Brady would revert to form of being little more than talk."

"And Roy Amory wanted to be prepared." Sean rubbed his eyes briefly. "Jesus Christ."

Jennifer said, "So it was Roy Amory who blew that school? Not Albert Brady."

Belamy had the decency to at last lower his eyes. "I'm afraid that's right, yes."

Jennifer demanded, "Then tell us this, Belamy. Did you know all this then? Before it actually happened?"

"Of course not. I wouldn't have let those children die."

"Then how the holy hell can you claim to know it all now?" Sean demanded.

"Because Roy told me."

For a moment Jennifer wasn't sure she'd heard him correctly. "Did you just say Roy Amory confessed his part in that Beardsly massacre straight out?"

"I did, Agent Bennett. I'm so sorry."

"Then why, if you have any human conscience at all, haven't you exposed him before now?"

Belamy hooked an arm around his chair. With his free hand, he picked up his coffee and sipped without answering until he'd drained his cup. "I couldn't," he answered simply.

"Why?"

"You cited the reason a moment ago yourself, my dear."

"What are you talking about?"

"He confessed."

Sean dropped his head back to briefly stare at the ceiling while he ran his hands through his hair. He looked at Belamy. "Something compelled him to come to you in the aftermath after all, at which point he told you everything in the spirit of supplicant to father confessor."

"That's right, Agent Alexander. You see, my hands were tied."

Jennifer looked to Sean, only after a moment understanding the full weight of the spirit of the doctrine the two men, so opposed in their basic religious beliefs, were referencing.

Sean saw the understanding in her eyes. "Any words or conversations that pass in a confessional exchange are binding. Whatever Roy Amory told Phillip Belamy after the bombing of Beardsly could never be revealed in the spirit of that binding trust."

Belamy was nodding. "That's right. Because the secrets of the confessional are sacred."

"But you've broken that trust now," Jennifer pointed out. "Why?"

Belamy shrugged. "As I said, my dear, I *do* have a conscious, and the Lattimore kidnapping has made national news. Besides that," he hesitated.

"What?"

"Well, it isn't as though I'm a Catholic."

Ten thirty-five a.m.

Roy saw the dark sedan almost as soon as he pulled into the company parking lot. But the two men in suits weren't inside the car this morning. Which meant they clearly were inside the building, though it was early, asking about him. What did they want to know specifically?

Was he a good worker? Was he a law-abiding citizen? Was he the kind of person who would have beaten his wife and dog if he'd had them? Dammit, they had no *right* to pry. They had no right to show up now, getting between him and his son. He thought of the talisman inside his desk drawer. Sam, I need you! But he couldn't get to him, couldn't touch him.

For a numbing moment, he felt as if he were losing Sam all over again . . . and then he knew. This was another sign!

Sam had finally ascended. There was nothing else of him *left* on earth to clasp. Which meant it was time to offer the new one. The other perfect boy who awaited him so quietly and patiently back at the house.

Smiling, filled with the sublime joy of understanding at last, Roy took one last earthly look at his office building and turned his car around.

Got you, you cocksucker! Ben was smiling, too, as he trailed Roy out of the lot.

"Sean!" Both Sean and Jennifer turned to the conference room door at the intrusion. Arty Hopkins said, "I'm sorry to interrupt this, but," he gestured to them both to step outside.

"Please, you two, I don't mind," Belamy assured them. He got up and helped himself to another cup of coffee from the machine plugged in on the credenza behind him. Jennifer and Sean watched him actually start to whistle as he poured. More than disgusted, they stepped outside, closing the conference room door behind them.

Hopkins handed Sean three computerized sheets. They were copies of contractual agreements. While Sean started to scan one, and Jennifer leaned in close to read across his shoulder, Hopkins explained, "A run of all the real estate agencies in our metropolitan and surrounding areas turned up twenty-seven hits of possible renters or buyers of rural property within the last six months. There were no Amory's, and two of the contracts you have were negotiated by clients named Roy."

"But it's this third that excites you," Sean supplied, scanning the contract whose client wasn't named Roy.

"Yeah, there's just something about the syntax, I don't know. What do you think?"

"Andy Ross," Jennifer said, reading aloud the name on the signature line. "Hancock County. Where's that?"

"East of the city," Hopkins replied. "Lots of farm-land out there. Lots of—"

"Country," Sean said. "Arty, baby-sit Belamy in there. I'm calling the team together with all the necessary backup. Of the three, we're heading for this Andy Ross first. My gut tells me you're right, that it's Amory. If it is, he's going down now."

Jennifer was already in front of Sean, heading for the door.

Roy cut his engine in the driveway and sat in the car for a moment, gathering himself. It was all so overwhelming, what He had charged him to do. But do it he would. He hadn't failed at Beardsly, even though he'd been called upon God to carry through the sacrifice, in the style of Abraham, of his beloved only son.

And in this, the second test, he wouldn't fail his God now.

Charlie scrambled off the bed when he heard the car engine shut off in the driveway and, moments later, the hateful key scrape in the basement door lock. It was way too early for the man to be home. Which told Charlie he was home for a reason. For a purpose. *Daddy*, he thought, not realizing he was hugging himself, *I don't want to die.*

＊　　＊　　＊

He wouldn't use the gun yet. First, he'd take this time to say good-bye. To so many things, he was bidding farewell. The ten million dollars for which he'd negotiated. Even the showdown with Sean Alexander, the planning to which he'd dedicated the past year of his life.

It didn't matter. God was speaking to him, and before Him all petty human wishes and desires dissolved as dust.

"Charlie, son," he called down into the dimness of the final place that awaited him, "I'm home!"

He began descending the steps.

Having entered the house behind Roy through the unlocked kitchen door, Ben waited until Roy was down the basement steps. Then he pulled out his pistol and, soundlessly, passed through the open basement door, too.

Sean and Jennifer, both suited in federal protective gear, adjusted the fit of their bullet-resistant vests. They were sitting with O'Brien and Clemm, identically suited, in the back of the state police SWAT vehicle that raced them east of Indianapolis. No one talked, because each in his own way was dealing with the slow burn of adrenaline that always accompanied a raid.

Jennifer did glance down at her watch once, commenting, "It's almost noon." Sean watched her while his long body swayed easily with the motion of the van.

The other agents looked at him, saying nothing. They all knew that if fortune was with them, the safe resolution they sought would be achieved well before six this evening. They also had too much experience not to know that sometimes the best laid plans didn't need a logical reason to go wrong.

Why was he crying? Roy wondered. They were both about to experience Glory, what could be wrong? "Charlie, come over here, let me comfort you, my son." He held out his arms, waiting for the boy to surrender. Then Charlie's eyes went wide. A scream that never sounded materialized on the boy's lips.

"Charlie, *wha*—!"

The blow of Ben Keaghan's gun opened a gash in the back of Roy Amory's head, dropping him, stunned, to the floor.

Charlie didn't think the tall dark man who rushed down the last few steps to attack his kidnapper even realized a little boy, a silent witness, was standing there. He just kept snarling something unintelligible as he hit the kidnapper over and over again with the sharp-edged metal of his gun.

Charlie was horrified and sickened at the sight of the spraying blood. It covered not only the kidnapper's face, but also the shirt of the crazy man who started smiling as he continued to rip the kidnapper's face.

"Who's the bad man now, Roy!" Charlie heard the crazy man yell. "Who's on his knees now? Is this where you had Hal? Is this how you had my sister before you tried to kill her? *Hm?*"

The kidnapper, despite the viciousness he couldn't escape, was crawling across the floor, closer to Charlie, closer to the bed. And still, Charlie could only stand gulping in dry sobs.

Away from the stairs, Charlie realized! He suddenly looked beyond the horror and saw his way out. In a burst of speed to which both men were oblivious, Charlie Lattimore broke into a run.

Paul Lattimore was sitting in his study, his chin in his hands, when the ringing telephone made him jump. He reached across his desk and snatched it up. "Hello."

"Daddy, help me, *help* me!"

Lattimore went hot then cold. "Charlie! Oh my God, my *God*. Where *are* you?"

* * *

"Agent Alexander?" The police officer riding shot-gun beside the vehicle driver passed his phone back to Sean.

Again, all eyes in the back of the van turned to him. Immediately, everyone sat up a little straighter, instantly on alert as Sean murmured urgently and low, "That's it, then. Arty, thanks." He disconnected and looked up at his team. "Charlie Lattimore's alive." To the driver over his shoulder, he ordered. "Take this vehicle up to maximum—"

"I'm already driving maximum. I'll keep us safely on the road if you'll just leave the job of driving in my hands."

Sean eyed the speedometer and knew at least twenty extra miles per hour of speed could be pulled out cleanly with minimum risk. In a tone only he knew was deceptively calm, he said, "Move this god-damned vehicle now."

"You can't—"

"Because if you don't, I'll climb up there and move it myself after I've kicked your obstructing ass."

There were several waiting moments of silence inside the van.

The speedometer started to climb.

So much blood and sweat rolled into his eyes, Roy thought he was going blind. But he couldn't give into that panic because the stronger fear was for his life.

Ben Keaghan was going to kill him. Unless he could manage to . . . he crawled some more, closer to Charlie's bed and the dinner tray he'd forgotten to retrieve last night.

"—show you who's in charge here!" Ben was panting with effort now. "I'll kill you, for what you've done, kill you dead, Roy." He followed Roy's shivering crawling form to a squat little table beside the bed. "*Kill* you!"

By feel alone, Roy raised his blood streaked hand to the tabletop, to the tray, groping . . . until his fingers closed around what he wanted. Still calculating as he felt his senses going dim, Roy suddenly let his body go boneless, which wasn't hard to do. He managed to twist around to his back as he slid to the floor.

Ben Keaghan stopped. Was he dead? Roy's face was turned away, so he couldn't tell if his eyes were open or not. He leaned down.

Roy jabbed the sharp tines of the fork as hard and deep as he could into Ben Keaghan's face and twisted. The screaming man's blood dripped down to mingle with his own as Roy rolled out from beneath Keaghan's collapsing body.

Energized, Roy scrambled to claim what Keaghan had lost.

Using his sleeve to wipe his face, Roy got to his

knees and grabbed Ben's pistol in a two-handed grip. "Ben," he ordered softly, "look up."

Ben Keaghan thought, *"Bastard!"* before a single slug from his own gun destroyed what was left of his damaged face.

Charlie screamed at the sound of the gunshot. He heard his father demand, "Charlie's what's happening! Wha—" when he whirled around. And screamed again.

The blood-soaked monster who swayed in the basement doorway grinned at him while still gripping the gun he had just used to kill.

"Charlie, put the phone down."

If they hadn't seen the two cars in the driveway, Sean and the others would have thought the house was deserted. It was that quiet in the warm, motionless air of the afternoon. It was twenty minutes of two.

The doors of the SWAT van opened quickly and silently. The agents and police officers inside scattered until they had efficiently surrounded the house.

The SWAT commander looked at Sean, who was hunkered down beside the vehicle and, like him, out of a clear line of fire. Sean nodded.

The commander put his bullhorn to his mouth. "Roy Amory, your house and these premises are surrounded by the FBI and police. Come out with your hands up. Surrender yourself and the boy. *Now.*"

No, Roy thought! It was too soon. He speared Charlie with a wild stare while the boy trembled and stared back. If he didn't go outside, would they rush the house to take him? To kill him?

No! Only God had the right to take him to heaven, if that was His will today. The decision of whether he lived or died would *not* be left to the hands of man. He rushed Charlie, who drew back against the counter so hard he stumbled. Roy grabbed him by the scruff of the neck.

"Come on, boy, they want us outside? We're going out."

As Sean watched Amory and Charlie Lattimore emerge from the house, he experienced a weird déjà vu. For a split second, he was looking into the mad face of Albert Brady. For an even wilder instant, the features of Samuel Amory superimposed themselves over those of Paul Lattimore's son.

And then Amory was screaming.

"Alexander! I want you now or the boy dies right now, right here!"

Sean watched Amory shake Charlie so hard the boy jerked back and forth against him like one of those rag dolls in Amory's strangely sterile house. He glanced at the SWAT commander.

"This bastard's a live one, Alexander. What's your call?"

Sean turned his eyes back to Charlie, watched him being shaken again. There was only one call. History had made it. "I'm stepping in." He stood up and left the cover of the van.

Roy Amory heard himself gasp as he actually looked his son's killer in the face. How could Alexander appear so controlled, so untouched when his own world had crumbled in a sleepy little town beside the Pacific Ocean.

He looked down at Charlie Lattimore's blond head. Who was *this* boy?

"Roy, you have nowhere to go," Sean said. "Release the boy, and this can all end right now."

"That's what you told Albert and look what happened to *him*."

Hearing and seeing how completely the man had snapped, Sean answered, "Albert didn't want to cooperate. He caused that situation—that explosion that killed your son and all the others. But you won't make that mistake, will you, Roy? You're smarter than Albert was."

Roy stared at Sean balefully for a long, tense moment. Then without warning, put the barrel of Ben Keaghan's pistol to Charlie Lattimore's head.

*　　*　　*

Sean thought his heart actually stopped. But with steely effort, he kept the expression on his face neutral while it started beating again. Out of the corner of his eye, he saw Jennifer, positioned somewhere behind him and still under cover of the van, ease her way closer to him while staying down.

"Roy, you don't really want to hurt this boy, do you? I know what you believe. I know how you value children's lives. That's why I know you want to keep Charlie safe."

Roy said nothing, but he listened intently.

"It's me who you're angry with, so just let Charlie go and you and I, just the two of us, will talk this thing out."

"How do I know this isn't a trick?"

"I'm not wearing a gun." He thought of the one holstered out of sight, in the small of his back. "You can see that. I have no way to stop you from hurting me if you want to, or Charlie for that matter. Doesn't that prove to you that what I'm telling you is in good faith?"

Roy's gun waivered.

The spit was still dry inside Sean's mouth.

Without warning, Roy's gun firmed up again. "I listened once to your lying mouth, Alexander!"

Every officer and agent close enough to the man and boy could actually hear the whimper that came out of Charlie Lattimore's open mouth. Every cop and agent out of hearing distance *thought* he heard that sound as they watched Charlie's panic and saw the resolution in Roy Amory's eyes.

Time suddenly slowed for Sean. He moved his hand.

"Roy, wait!" Jennifer stepped out from beside the van taking Roy, Sean, and several others watching the exchange by surprise. "Look, I'm not lying." She held her pistol out in front of her and dropped it to the ground. "Okay? Can we talk? After all it's me you wanted to meet in the park. At least give me this moment with you now."

Amory continued to clutch Charlie, glaring at Jennifer, his face a gruesome mask of bloody concentration.

"I know what it's like to watch someone you love die."

Sean, surprised at that, listened closely along with Amory.

Amory said, "You do not, you're just making that up to trick me."

"No, Roy, I'm not."

Roy seemed to subtly lose a small measure of his rigidity. "Was it your child, then?" His voice had fallen to a near whisper. "Did you have a little baby die?"

"No, Roy. It's my grandfather."

Sean watched Jennifer, startled. She was negotiating with a madman, but he believed with certainty the leverage she was using was in no way pretend.

"He isn't dead yet, Roy. But he's dying and there's nothing I can do to stop it. I could lash out at the doctors who only give him a few months to live. I could curse the God that gave him the disease that's killing him. But it would do neither me nor him any good if I did any of that."

"No good?" Roy's gun slipped away again from Charlie's head.

Sean smoothly began to back away from where he was standing. He gave Jennifer center stage, visually, for Amory's sake, ceding to her control of the situation.

"No good," Roy repeated. And to everyone's surprise, let the gun drop to his side.

"Do you believe me, Roy?" Jennifer asked, softly gesturing with a half raised hand to Charlie. She was motioning him to start walking away. "Hm?" she pressed.

"No good," Roy murmured yet again. Then he started softly crying.

Jennifer watched the sobs physically rack the killer in front of her. And was amazed to realize that despite knowing what he was, she couldn't remain completely unmoved by his abject pain and tears. Was this what Sean had felt that day in front of the schoolhouse, confronted with another madman whose heart was breaking?

"Come on, Charlie, it's okay," Jennifer urged. "Just keep walking out."

Charlie Lattimore moved as carefully and slowly as if he were walking through a minefield. Jennifer watched him make it closer and closer to her and the van. She was already holding out a hand to him, listening to Amory chant, "No good."

Which was how she missed the implacable change in Amory's tear-drenched eyes.

Sean didn't, and never felt his hand moving to the back of his waist. He only heard the crack of Roy Amory's pistol, saw the little puff of dust that snapped up beside Charlie Lattimore's feet. Saw Jennifer's horrified face as Roy aimed his gun again at the boy.

"Charlie, get down!" Jennifer screamed. Two SWAT shooters were suddenly on their stomachs in front of the van, their rifles aimed at Amory.

"No!" Roy Amory screamed again before another shot rent the air and a red stain blossomed across his chest.

The SWAT marksmen looked around in confusion. None of them had fired. Then they looked behind them.

Sean Alexander was standing there, his drawn gun lowering to his side. A hard look etched faint lines Jennifer hadn't noticed around his mouth and under his stony eyes more deeply.

*　　*　　*

Another vehicle, a long dark car, pulled up imposingly into the driveway behind the others. Neither Jennifer nor Sean paid immediate attention to the three men who emerged.

Jennifer reached Sean's side. He didn't look at her. He continued to stare at the body of Roy Amory, already looking alone and forgotten in the leaves and grass in which it lay.

Since he wouldn't look at her, she took his hand. "Sean, you saved a life," she told him softly. "Your instincts allowed you to see what was true, and you only did what was demanded. Charlie Lattimore is alive because of you."

As if on cue, she heard Charlie's young excited voice ring out, "Daddy!"

And at last, Sean emitted a heartfelt sigh and looked down at her.

His expression seemed to search for something. She moved closer to him—and stepped inside his wordlessly opened arms.

At a short distance from Sean and Jennifer where a man and reunited son embraced, a team of police officers went about their grim business of seeing to the dead. The two men at the limo observed them and accepted that fact like the seasoned professionals they were. Then they returned their attention to the two agents still embracing, clearly oblivious to anything but themselves.

"Well, Gerry, looks like your intuition is as uncanny as ever, still right on target." Anthony Collins rested one hand on the wheelchair beside him, and used his other to lift a forbidden cigarette to his lips.

"Not intuition, just long-term observation and a healthy dose of the common sense that should accompany it. I told you I wanted the best for my granddaughter." He narrowed his eyes, watching the couple in the distance. "With your help, I think I just may have gotten it."

Collins gazed, along with Gerard Bennett, at the two agents who broke apart after finally sensing they were being watched.

"I got what I wanted, too," Collins told his friend as Sean and Jennifer approached them. Two of the best, together on his watch, both working for him and for the bureau in the prime of their capabilities.

And there was, Collins thought, something very much together about them although they merely squeezed each other's hands before letting go.

"Grandad," Jennifer said smiling intimately. She leaned down to embrace Gerard Bennett, then gently disengaged herself to stand at his side. "Here's someone I'd like you to meet." She turned to Sean.

"Sir, it's an honor." Sean stepped forward, extending his hand.

Gerry Bennett nodded, measuring. Then, still saying nothing, he reached out to accept Sean Alexander's gesture with a small private smile.

SIGNET

DANIEL HECHT

"Accomplished...SKULL SESSION is a story that keeps the reader guessing till the very end."—*New York Times Book Review*

"SKULL SESSION is the most psychologically sophisticated thriller I've read since THE ALIENIST."—Stephen White, author of HARM'S WAY

SKULL SESSION

A young man suffering from Tourette's Syndrome desperately searches for steady work before his ex-wife can claim custody of their son. He accepts a job offer from his eccentric aunt to repair her old Hudson Valley mansion, and takes his girlfriend along to help. Sifting through the rubble, he discovers that the house has been vandalized by an almost superhuman rage. And when dead teenagers are found in the area, the violent path leads directly to the mansion's door. To end the horror, he must confront his family's past, and the dark side of his own soul....

☐0-451-19592-2/$6.99

Prices slightly higher in Canada

Payable in U.S. funds only. No cash/COD accepted. Postage & handling: U.S./CAN. $2.75 for one book, $1.00 for each additional, not to exceed $6.75; Int'l $5.00 for one book, $1.00 each additional. We accept Visa, Amex, MC ($10.00 min.), checks ($15.00 fee for returned checks) and money orders. Call 800-788-6262 or 201-933-9292, fax 201-896-8569; refer to ad # HECHT

Penguin Putnam Inc.
P.O. Box 12289, Dept. B
Newark, NJ 07101-5289
Please allow 4-6 weeks for delivery.
Foreign and Canadian delivery 6-8 weeks.

Bill my: ☐Visa ☐MasterCard ☐Amex_____(expires)
Card#_____

Signature_____

Bill to:

Name_____
Address_____City_____
State/ZIP_____
Daytime Phone #_____

Ship to:

Name_____ Book Total $_____
Address_____ Applicable Sales Tax $_____
City_____ Postage & Handling $_____
State/ZIP_____ Total Amount Due $_____

This offer subject to change without notice.